To: BECKY
FROM: GERALDINE
XMAS 2002

Favourite Story Collection

SELECTED BY ALISON SAGE

HUTCHINSON

LONDON SYDNEY AUCKLAND JOHANNESBURG

CONTENTS

Nicola Bayley
NURSERY RHYMES

GOOSEY, goosey, gander,
Whither shall I wander?
Upstairs and downstairs
And in my lady's chamber.
There I met an old man
Who would not say his prayers,
I took him by the left leg
And threw him down the stairs.

THIS little pig went to market,
This little pig stayed at home,
This little pig had roast beef,
And this little pig had none,
And this little pig went wee–wee–wee
all the way home.

THERE was an old woman
Who lived in a shoe,
She had so many children
She didn't know what to do;
She gave them some broth
Without any bread,
And whipped them all soundly
And put them to bed.

THERE was a crooked man,
And he walked a crooked mile,
He found a crooked sixpence
Against a crooked stile;
He bought a crooked cat,
Which caught a crooked mouse,
And they all lived together
In a little crooked house.

THE QUEEN OF HEARTS

Illustrated by Randolph Caldecott

T HE Queen of Hearts,
She made some Tarts,

All on a Summer's Day:

The Knave of Hearts,

He stole those Tarts,
And took them right away.

The King of Hearts,
Called for those Tarts,
And beat the Knave full sore:

The Knave of Hearts,
Brought back those Tarts,

And vowed he'd steal no more.

Quentin Blake
NURSERY RHYME BOOK

LITTLE Jack Sprat
Once had a pig,
It was not very little,
Nor yet very big,
It was not very lean,
It was not very fat –
It's a good pig to grunt,
Said little Jack Sprat.

PUSSY Cat ate the dumplings,
Pussy Cat ate the dumplings,
Mama stood by,
And cried, Oh fie!
Why did you eat
the dumplings?

HANDY spandy, Jack-a-Dandy
Loves plum cake and sugar candy.
He bought some at a grocer's shop

And out he came,
 hop, hop,
  hop, hop!

NURSERY RHYME CLASSICS

Illustrated by Kate Greenaway

Mary had a little lamb,
Its fleece was white as snow;
And everywhere that Mary went
The lamb was sure to go.

It followed her to school one day,
Which was against the rule;
It made the children laugh and play
To see a lamb at school.

And so the teacher sent it out,
But still it waited near;
And stood there patiently about
Till Mary did appear.

"Why does the lamb love Mary so?"
The eager children cry;
"Why, Mary loves the lamb, you know,"
The teacher did reply.

A dillar, a dollar,
  A ten o'clock scholar,
What makes you come so soon?
You used to come at ten o'clock
But now you come at noon.

ONE foot up and one foot down
This is the way to London Town.

JACK Sprat could eat no fat
His wife could eat no lean
And so between them both, you see,
They licked the platter clean.

RING-a-ring-a-roses
A pocket full of posies.
Atishoo! Atishoo!
We all fall down.

Picking up the daisies
Picking up the daisies.
Atishoo! Atishoo!
We all stand up.

"Pussy cat, pussy cat, where have you been?"
    "I've been up to London to visit the Queen."
"Pussy cat, pussy cat, what did you there?"
"I frightened a little mouse under her chair."

MOTHER GOOSE

Illustrated by Arthur Rackham

BAA, baa, black sheep,
Have you any wool?
"Yes, sir, yes, sir,
Three bags full:
One for my master,
And one for my dame,
And one for the little boy
Who lives in the lane."

BYE, baby bunting.
Daddy's gone a hunting,
To get a little rabbit's skin
To wrap the baby bunting in.

HERE we go round the mulberry bush,
The mulberry bush, the mulberry bush,
Here we go round the mulberry bush,
On a cold and frosty morning.

This is the way we wash our hands,
Wash our hands, wash our hands,
This is the way we wash our hands,
On a cold and frosty morning.

This is the way we wash our clothes,
Wash our clothes, wash our clothes,
This is the way we wash our clothes,
On a cold and frosty morning.

This is the way we go to school,
Go to school, go to school,
This is the way we go to school,
On a cold and frosty morning.

This is the way we come out of school,
Come out of school, come out of school,
This is the way we come out of school,
On a cold and frosty morning.

Goldilocks and the Three Bears

TRADITIONAL ~ RETOLD BY ANN MACLEOD AND
ILLUSTRATED BY WENDY SMITH

ONCE UPON A TIME there were three bears who lived together in a pretty little cottage in the middle of a wood. There was a Little Tiny Wee Bear, a Middle-Sized Bear, and a Great Big Huge Bear. Now these bears were very fond of porridge and they each had their own porridge bowl: a little bowl for the Little Tiny Wee Bear, a middle-sized bowl for the Middle-Sized Bear and a big bowl for the Great Big Huge Bear. And they each had a chair to sit on: a little chair for the Little Tiny Wee Bear, a middle-sized chair for the Middle-Sized Bear and a big chair for the Great Big Huge Bear. And they each had a bed to sleep in: a little bed for the Little Tiny Wee Bear, a middle-sized bed for the Middle-Sized Bear and a big bed for the Great Big Huge Bear.

One fine summer morning when the Middle-Sized Bear had made the porridge and poured it into the three porridge bowls, the three bears decided to go for a walk in the wood while the porridge cooled, for they did not like burning their tongues by eating the porridge when it was too hot. So away they went through the wood – the Middle-Sized Bear and the Great Big Huge Bear walking along slowly while the Little Tiny Wee Bear ran in front and turned somersaults because it was such a beautiful morning.

While the three bears were out walking a little girl called Goldilocks came running through the wood. She stopped in surprise when she saw

the pretty little cottage and she stood on tiptoe and peered in the window. Seeing nobody inside, she turned the door handle. The door opened and in walked Goldilocks.

Now Goldilocks was not a very nice little girl or she would never have walked into another person's house without being invited. And now, when she saw the porridge on the table, she felt hungry and decided to have some herself, which again was not a very nice thing to do.

First she tasted the porridge in the big bowl but that was too salty for her. Then she tasted the porridge in the middle-sized bowl but that was too sweet for her. And then she tasted the porridge in the little bowl and that was just right, and Goldilocks liked it so much that she ate it all up.

Then Goldilocks sat down in the big chair and that was too hard for her. Then she sat down in the middle-sized chair and that was too soft for her. And then she sat down in the little chair and that was just right. But she sat herself down with such a bump that the bottom came out of the chair and Goldilocks fell through on to the floor.

Then Goldilocks went upstairs to the bedroom where the three bears slept. First she lay down on the big bed but that was too high at the head for her. Then she lay down on the middle-sized bed but that was too high at the foot for her. And then she lay down on the little bed and that was just right. So Goldilocks covered herself up with blankets and lay there comfortably until she fell fast asleep.

Soon the three bears came home to breakfast, and the first thing they saw was the three spoons standing in the three porridge bowls.

"Someone's been eating my porridge," said the Great Big Huge Bear in his great rough gruff voice.

"Someone's been eating my porridge," said the Middle-Sized Bear in her middle-sized voice.

"Someone's been eating my porridge and has eaten it all up!" squeaked the Little Tiny Wee Bear in his little tiny wee voice.

The three Bears began to look around the room.

"Someone's been sitting in my chair," said the Great Big Huge Bear in his great rough gruff voice.

"Someone's been sitting in my chair," said the Middle-Sized Bear in her middle-sized voice.

"Someone's been sitting in my chair and has broken the bottom out of it!" squeaked the Little Tiny Wee Bear in his little tiny wee voice, and he burst into tears.

The Middle-Sized Bear put a cushion across the broken seat and gave the Little Tiny Wee Bear some of her porridge so he stopped crying, and when the Great Big Huge Bear had made sure that there was nobody hiding in the kitchen the three bears went upstairs to their bedroom.

"Someone's been lying on my bed," said the Great Big Huge Bear in his great rough gruff voice.

"Someone's been lying on my bed too," said the Middle-Sized Bear in her middle-sized voice.

"Someone's been lying on my bed and she's still there!" squeaked the Little Tiny Wee Bear in his little tiny wee voice.

Goldilocks had heard in her sleep the rough gruff voice of the Great Big Huge Bear and the middle-sized voice of the Middle-Sized Bear, but only as if she had heard someone speaking in a dream. When she heard the little tiny wee voice of the Little Tiny Wee Bear it was so sharp and shrill that it wakened her at once. When she saw the three bears standing at one side of the bed she tumbled out of the other side and jumped out of the window. Then she ran away through the wood as fast as she could, and the three bears never saw her again.

Henny-Penny

TRADITIONAL ~ RETOLD BY JOSEPH JACOBS AND
ILLUSTRATED BY NICHOLAS ALLAN

ONE DAY HENNY-PENNY was picking up corn in the cornyard when — whack! — something hit her upon her head. "Goodness gracious me!" said Henny-Penny. "The sky's a-going to fall; I must go and tell the King."

So she went along and she went along, and she went along till she met Cocky-Locky. "Where are you going, Henny-Penny?" said Cocky-Locky.

"Oh! I'm going to tell the King the sky's a-falling," said Henny-Penny.

"May I come with you?" said Cocky-Locky.

"Certainly," said Henny-Penny. So Henny-Penny and Cocky-Locky went to tell the King the sky was a-falling.

They went along, and they went along, and they went along till they met Ducky-Daddles. "Where are you going to, Henny-Penny and Cocky-Locky?" said Ducky-Daddles.

"Oh! We're going to tell the King the sky's a-falling," said Henny-Penny and Cocky-Locky.

"May I come with you?" said Ducky-Daddles.

"Certainly," said Henny-Penny and Cocky-Locky. So Henny-Penny, Cocky-Locky and Ducky-Daddles went to tell the King the sky was a-falling.

So they went along, and they went along, and they went along, till they met Goosey-Poosey. "Where are you going to, Henny-Penny, Cocky-Locky and Ducky-Daddles?" said Goosey-Poosey.

"Oh! We're going to tell the King the sky's a-falling," said Henny-Penny and Cocky-Locky and Ducky-Daddles.

"May I come with you?" said Goosey-Poosey.

"Certainly," said Henny-Penny, Cocky-Locky and Ducky-Daddles. So Henny-Penny, Cocky-Locky, Ducky-Daddles and Goosey-Poosey went to tell the King the sky was a-falling.

So they went along, and they went along, and they went along, till they met Turkey-Lurkey. "Where are you going, Henny-Penny, Cocky-Locky, Ducky-Daddles and Goosey-Poosey?" said Turkey-Lurkey.

"Oh! We're going to tell the King the sky's a-falling," said Henny-Penny, Cocky-Locky, Ducky-Daddles and Goosey-Poosey.

"May I come with you, Henny-Penny, Cocky-Locky, Ducky-Daddles and Goosey-Poosey?" said Turkey-Lurkey.

"Oh, certainly, Turkey-Lurkey," said Henny-Penny, Cocky-Locky, Ducky-Daddles and Goosey-Poosey. So Henny-Penny, Cocky-Locky, Ducky-Daddles, Goosey-Poosey and Turkey-Lurkey all went to tell the King the sky was a-falling.

So they went along, and they went along, and they went along, and they went along, till they met Foxy-Woxy; and Foxy-Woxy said to Henny-Penny, Cocky-Locky, Ducky-Daddles, Goosey-Poosey and Turkey-Lurkey, "Where are you going, Henny-Penny, Cocky-Locky, Ducky-Daddles, Goosey-Poosey and Turkey-Lurkey?"

And Henny-Penny, Cocky-Locky, Ducky-Daddles, Goosey-Poosey and Turkey-Lurkey said to Foxy-Woxy: "We're going to tell the King the sky's a-falling."

"Oh! But this is not the way to the King, Henny-Penny, Cocky-Locky, Ducky-Daddles, Goosey-Poosey and Turkey-Lurkey," said Foxy-Woxy. "I know the proper way; shall I show it to you?"

"Oh, certainly, Foxy-Woxy," said Henny-Penny, Cocky-Locky, Ducky-Daddles, Goosey-Poosey and Turkey-Lurkey. So Henny-Penny, Cocky-Locky, Ducky-Daddles, Goosey-Poosey, Turkey-Lurkey and Foxy-Woxy all went to tell the King the sky was a-falling.

So they went along, and they went along, and they went along, till they came to a narrow and dark hole. Now this was the door of Foxy-Woxy's cave. But Foxy-Woxy said to Henny-Penny, Cocky-Locky, Ducky-Daddles, Goosey-Poosey and Turkey-Lurkey: "This is the short way to the King's palace; you'll soon get there if you follow me. I will go first and you come after, Henny-Penny, Cocky-Locky, Ducky-Daddles, Goosey-Poosey and Turkey-Lurkey."

"Why of course, certainly, without doubt, why not?" said Henny-Penny, Cocky-Locky, Ducky-Daddles, Goosey-Poosey and Turkey-Lurkey.

So Foxy-Woxy went into his cave, and he didn't go very far, but turned round to wait for Henny-Penny, Cocky-Locky, Ducky-Daddles, Goosey-Poosey and Turkey-Lurkey. At last Turkey-Lurkey went through the dark hole into the cave. She hadn't got far when "Hrumph!" Foxy-Woxy

caught Turkey-Lurkey and threw her over his left shoulder. Then Goosey-Poosey went in, and "Hrumph!" Goosey-Poosey was thrown beside Turkey-Lurkey. Then Ducky-Daddles waddled down, and "Hrumph!" Foxy-Woxy chased and caught Ducky-Daddles and threw him alongside Turkey-Lurkey and Goosey-Poosey.

Then Cocky-Locky strutted down into the cave, and he hadn't gone far when "Hrumph!" Cocky-Locky was thrown alongside Turkey-Lurkey, Goosey-Poosey and Ducky-Daddles.

But Cocky-Locky called out to Henny-Penny. And Henny-Penny turned tail and off she ran home; so she never did tell the King the sky was a-falling.

Nicholas Alla

The Three Little Pigs

TRADITIONAL ~ ILLUSTRATED BY ROB LEWIS

ONCE UPON A TIME there lived an old sow who had three little piglets, and as soon as they were old enough she sent them out into the world to seek their fortunes.

The first little pig met a man carrying a bundle of straw.

"Please, sir, give me that straw to build a house with," said the first little pig. The man gave him the straw and the little pig set to work to build himself a house. It wasn't very strong but it looked good.

No sooner had he finished it than along came a big grey wolf who knocked at the door of the little straw house and said, "Little pig, little pig, let me come in."

"No, no, no, not by the hairs of my chinny chin chin," squeaked the little pig in a great fright.

"Then I'll huff and I'll puff and I'll blow your house in," growled the wolf, and he huffed and he puffed and he blew the house in and gobbled up the little pig.

The second little pig met a man carrying a bundle of sticks.

"Please, sir, give me those sticks to build a house with," said the second little pig. The man gave him the sticks and the little pig soon built himself a little house. It was stronger than the house of straw, but not that strong.

As soon as he was inside, along came the wolf and said, "Little pig, little pig, let me come in."

"No, no, no, not by the hairs of my chinny chin chin," squeaked the little pig, trembling.

"Then I'll huff and I'll puff and I'll blow your house in," growled the wolf, and he huffed and he puffed and he puffed and he huffed and he blew the house in and gobbled up the second little pig.

The third little pig was smarter than the others. He met a man carrying a load of bricks.

"Please, sir, give me those bricks to build a house with," said the third little pig. The man gave him the bricks and soon the little pig had built himself a fine strong house.

The wolf came along to his house too, and knocked on the door, saying, "Little pig, little pig, let me come in."

"No, no, no, not by the hairs of my chinny chin chin," squeaked the little pig, not at all frightened of the wolf.

"Then I'll huff and I'll puff and I'll blow your house in," growled the wolf, and he huffed and he puffed and he puffed and he huffed and he huffed and he puffed, but he could not blow the little brick house in.

So the wolf decided to use trickery. He sat back on his haunches and got his breath back, and then he said, "Little pig, would you like some fine big turnips?"

"Oh yes, I would," said the little pig.

"Then come with me to Farmer Brown's turnip field early tomorrow morning," said the wolf, "and we will collect enough for both of us. I'll come and fetch you at six o'clock."

"Very well," said the little pig, "I'll be ready for you."

But the little pig got up at five o'clock the next morning, and he went to the field, got a great sackful of turnips and was back in his house again before the wolf arrived.

"Little pig, are you ready?" asked the wolf.

"Ready?" answered the little pig. "Why, I've been and come back again and got a nice potful for dinner."

The wolf was very angry, but he made up his mind to catch the little pig somehow, so he said, "Little pig, would you like some nice sweet apples?"

"Yes I would," said the little pig.

"Then come down to the orchard with me tomorrow morning," said the wolf. "And as you get up so early I will call for you at five o'clock."

"I'll be ready," said the little pig.

But he got up at four o'clock and ran down to the orchard, hoping to get back before the wolf arrived. But the wolf had got up early too, and just as the little pig was climbing down the apple tree he saw the wolf coming into the orchard, which did frighten him.

"Are you here before me, little pig?" said the wolf. "And are they nice apples?"

"Yes, very," said the little pig. "I will throw you one down." And he threw it so far that, while the wolf ran down the hill to pick it up, the little pig jumped down from the tree and ran home.

The next day the wolf came again, and said to the little pig, "Little pig, there is a fair in the town this afternoon. Will you come?"

"Oh yes," said the little pig, "I will come. What time will you be ready?"

"At three o'clock," said the wolf.

So the little pig went off before the time, as usual, and got to the fair and bought a butter churn. He was on his way home with it when he saw the wolf coming towards him. So the little pig jumped into the butter churn to hide. The churn toppled over and the pig went rolling down the hill right behind the wolf. This frightened the wolf so much that he ran home without going to the fair.

He went to the little pig's house next day and told him how terrified he had been by a great round thing which came rolling down the hill towards him.

The little pig laughed and said, "Oh, did I frighten you? That was me in my brand new churn."

That made the wolf very angry indeed, and he jumped up on to the roof of the little house, snarling that he would get down the chimney to gobble up the little pig.

When the little pig saw what was happening he made up the fire until it was blazing hot and then he hung a great pot full of water over it. When the wolf came down the chimney the little pig lifted the lid off the pot and the wolf tumbled right into it. Then the little pig clapped the lid back on. And an hour later he gobbled the wolf up, with a scrumptious portion of turnips and apples on the side.

Tony Ross
I WANT MY POTTY

"NAPPIES ARE YUUECH!" said the little princess. "There MUST be something better!"

"The potty's the place," said the queen.

At first the little princess thought the potty was worse.

"THE POTTY'S THE PLACE!" said the queen.

So…the little princess had to learn.

Sometimes the little princess was a long way from the potty when she needed it most.

Sometimes the little princess played tricks on the potty…

…and sometimes the potty played tricks on the little princess.

Soon the potty was fun

and the little princess loved it.

Everybody said the little princess was clever and would grow up to be a wonderful queen.

"The potty's the place!" said the little princess proudly.

One day the little princess was playing at the top of the castle… when…

"I WANT MY POTTY!" she cried.

"She wants her potty," cried the maid.

"She wants her potty," cried the king.

"She wants her potty," cried the cook.

"She wants her potty," cried the gardener.

"She wants her potty," cried the general.

"I know where it is," cried the admiral.

So the potty was taken as quickly as possible to the little princess... just

...a little too late.

Ruth Brown

A DARK, DARK TALE

ONCE UPON A TIME there was a dark, dark moor. On the moor there was a dark, dark wood.

In the wood there was a dark, dark house.
At the front of the house there was a dark, dark door.

Behind the door there was a dark, dark hall.
In the hall there were some dark, dark stairs.

Up the stairs there was a dark, dark passage.
Across the passage was a dark, dark curtain.

Behind the curtain was a dark, dark room.
In the room was a dark, dark cupboard.

In the cupboard was a dark, dark corner.
In the corner was a dark, dark box.

And in the box there was …   **A MOUSE!**

PAT-A-CAKE, PAT-A-CAKE

Illustrated by Sarah Pooley

PAT-A-CAKE, pat-a-cake,
Baker's man,
Bake me a cake
As fast as you can.
Pat it and prick it
And mark it with B,
And put it in the oven
For Baby and me.

Shigeo Watanabe

HALLO! HOW ARE YOU?

Illustrated by Yasuo Ohtomo

"HALLO, FLOWERS. How are you?"

"Hallo, sparrows.
How are you?"

"Hallo, cat.
How are you?"

"Hallo, dog.
How are you?"

"Hallo, Mr Milkman.
How are you?"

"Hallo, Mr Paperman.
How are you?"

"Hallo, Mr Postman.
How are you?"

"Hallo, Mama.
How are you?"

"What a funny
little bear you are."

"Wait. Wait!"

"Hallo, Papa.
How are you?"

"Hallo, Little Bear.
I'm very well, thank you.
How are you?"

SING A
SONG OF SIXPENCE

Illustrated by Randolph Caldecott

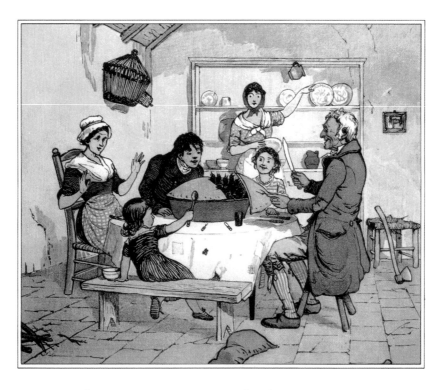

SING a song of sixpence,
A pocket full of rye;
Four and twenty blackbirds,
Baked in a pie.

When the pie was opened,
The birds began to sing.
Wasn't that a dainty dish,
To set before the king?

The king was in the counting house,
Counting out his money;
The queen was in the parlour,
Eating bread and honey;

The maid was in the garden
Hanging out the clothes,
When down came a blackbird
And snapped off her nose.

But then there came a Jenny wren
And popped it on again.

David McKee

KING ROLLO AND THE NEW SHOES

ONE DAY King Rollo visited the shoe shop.

He bought himself a new pair of shoes.

Of course, he already had shoes.

Kings have lots of shoes.

Lots and lots

and lots of shoes.

But King Rollo's new shoes were different.

His new shoes had laces.

King Rollo smiled and put on his new shoes.

"Do them up for me, please," he said to the magician.

"I can't always be around to do up your laces," said the magician.

"Make a magic spell to do them up," said King Rollo.

"A waste of magic. I'll show you how to do them up," said the magician.

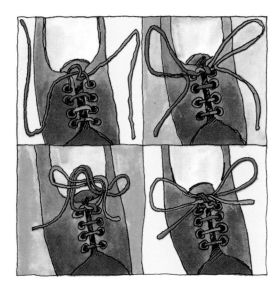

"Left over right and under and pull. Make a little loop. Now make another. One loop goes over and under the other."

He repeated it with the other shoe.

"Just practise," said the magician, as King Rollo went into his room.

Soon strange noises came from the room. "Left over right and under and BLOW!"

And sometimes a sudden CRASH! like a thrown shoe.

"King Rollo has new shoes," the magician told the cook. "Lace-ups."

Later the noises were much quieter.

That afternoon Queen Gwen came to have tea with King Rollo.

The cook took her to King Rollo's room just as he came out.

"Oh," said Queen Gwen. "I do like your new shoes – they're lace-ups.

"Yes," smiled King Rollo, "and I did them up myself."

John Burningham
MR GUMPY'S OUTING

T<small>HIS</small> is Mr Gumpy.

Mr Gumpy owned a boat and his house was by a river.

One day Mr Gumpy went out in his boat.
"May we come with you?" said the children.
"Yes," said Mr Gumpy, "if you don't squabble."
"Can I come along, Mr Gumpy?" said the rabbit.
"Yes, but don't hop about."
"I'd like a ride," said the cat.
"Very well," said Mr Gumpy. "But you're not to chase the rabbit."

"Will you take me with you?" said the dog.
"Yes," said Mr Gumpy. "But don't tease the cat."
"May I come, please, Mr Gumpy?" said the pig.
"Very well, but don't muck about."
"Have you a place for me?" said the sheep.
"Yes, but don't keep bleating."

"Can we come too?" said the chickens.
"Yes, but don't flap," said Mr Gumpy.
"Can you make room for me?" said the calf.
"Yes, if you don't trample about."
"May I join you, Mr Gumpy?" said the goat.
"Very well, but don't kick."

For a little while they all went
along happily but then …

The goat kicked

The calf trampled

The chickens flapped

The sheep bleated

The pig mucked about

The dog teased the cat

The cat chased the rabbit

The rabbit hopped

The children squabbled

The boat tipped …

and into the water they fell.

Then Mr Gumpy and the goat and the calf and the chickens and the sheep and the pig and the dog and the cat and the rabbit and the children all swam to the bank and climbed out to dry in the hot sun. "We'll walk home across the fields," said Mr Gumpy. "It's time for tea."

"Goodbye," said Mr Gumpy. "Come for a ride another day."

Shirley Hughes
ALFIE'S FEET

ALFIE HAD A LITTLE SISTER called Annie Rose. Alfie's feet were quite big. Annie Rose's feet were rather small. They were all soft and pink underneath. Alfie knew a game he could play with Annie Rose, counting her toes.

Annie Rose had lots of different ways of getting about. She went forwards, crawling, and backwards, on her behind, and she liked to slide about very fast on her potty, skidding round and round on the floor and in and out of the table legs.

Annie Rose had some new red shoes. She could walk in them a bit, if she was pushing her little cart or holding on to someone's hand.

When they went out, Annie Rose wore her red shoes and Alfie wore his old brown ones. Mum usually helped him put them on, because he wasn't very good at doing up the laces yet.

If it had been raining Alfie
liked to go stamping about
in mud and walking
through puddles,

splish, splash, SPLOSH!

Then his shoes got
rather wet.

So did his socks,

and so did his feet.

So one Saturday morning Alfie and Mum went to a big shop in the High Street.

They bought a pair of shiny new yellow boots for Alfie to wear when he went stamping about in mud and walking through puddles. Alfie was very pleased. He carried them home himself in a cardboard box.

When they got in, Alfie sat down at once and unwrapped his new boots. He put them on all by himself and walked about in them,

stamp! stamp! stamp!

He went into the kitchen to show Mum and Dad and Annie Rose, stamping his feet all the way,

stamp! stamp! stamp!

The boots were very smart and shiny but they felt funny.

Alfie wanted to go out again right away. So he put on his mac, and Dad took his book and his newspaper and they went off to the park.

Alfie stamped in a lot of mud and walked through a lot of puddles, splish, splash, SPLOSH! He frightened some sparrows who were having a bath. He even frightened two big ducks. They went hurrying back to their pond, walking with their feet turned in.

Alfie looked down at his feet. They still felt funny. They kept turning outwards. Dad was sitting on a bench. They both looked at Alfie's feet.

Suddenly Alfie knew what was wrong!

Dad lifted Alfie on to the bench beside him and helped him to take off each boot and put it on the other foot. And when Alfie stood down again his feet didn't feel a bit funny any more.

After tea Mum painted a big black R on to one of Alfie's
boots and a big black L on the other to help Alfie
remember which boot was which. The R was for Right
foot and the L was for Left foot. The black paint wore off
in the end and the boots stopped being new and shiny, but
Alfie usually did remember to get them on the proper way
round after that.

They felt much better when he
went stamping about in mud and
walking through puddles.

And, of course, Annie Rose made
such a fuss about Alfie having new
boots that she had to have a pair
of her own to go stamping
about in too,

splish, splash, SPLOSH!

HICKORY, DICKORY, DOCK

Illustrated by Sarah Pooley

Hickory, dickory, dock,
The mouse ran up the clock.
The clock struck one,
The mouse ran down,
Hickory, dickory, dock.
Tick tock, tick tock.

Hiawyn Oram
IN THE ATTIC

Illustrated by Satoshi Kitamura

I HAD A MILLION TOYS and I was bored.

I climbed into the attic.

I was there now. The attic was empty. Or was it?

I found a family of mice

94

and a colony of beetles and a cool, quiet place to rest and think.

I met a spider and we made a web.

I opened a window that opened other windows.

I found an old engine and I made it work.

I went out to look for someone to share what I had found

and found a friend. My friend and I

found a game that could go on forever because it kept changing.

I climbed out of the attic and told my mother where I'd been all day.

"But we don't have an attic," she said.

Well, she wouldn't know, would she?

She hasn't found the ladder.

Ezra Jack Keats
THE SNOWY DAY

ONE WINTER MORNING Peter woke up
and looked out of the window.
Snow had fallen during the night. It
covered everything as far as he could see.

After breakfast he put on his snowsuit and ran
outside. The snow was piled up very high
along the street to make a path for walking.

Crunch, crunch, crunch, his feet sank into the snow.
He walked with his toes pointing out, like this.

He walked with his toes pointing in, like that.
Then he dragged his feet s-l-o-w-l-y to make tracks.

And he found something sticking out
of the snow that made a new track. It was a stick

— a stick that was just right for
smacking a snow-covered tree.
Down fell the snow – plop!
– on top of Peter's head.

He thought it would be fun to join the big boys in their snowball fight, but he knew he wasn't old enough – not yet.

So he made a smiling snowman, and he made angels.

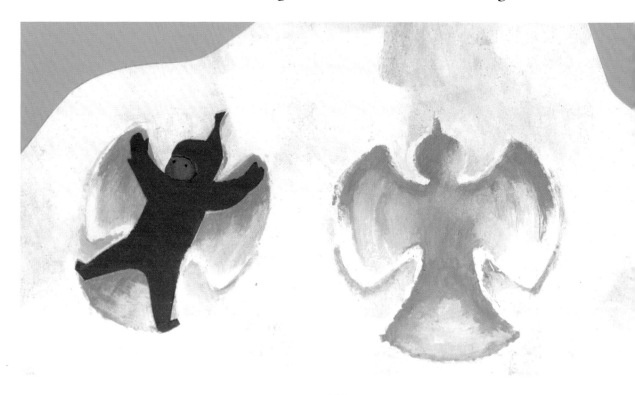

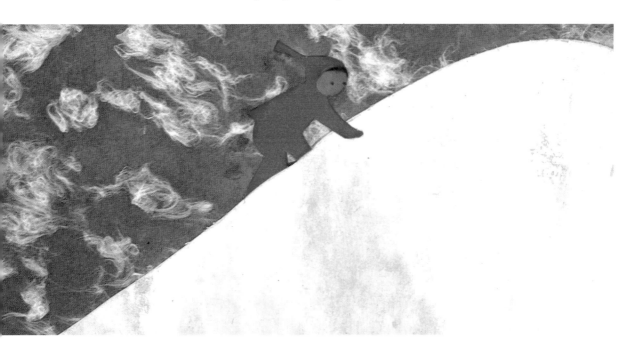

He pretended he was a mountain-climber.
He climbed up a great big tall heaping mountain of snow –

and slid all the way down.

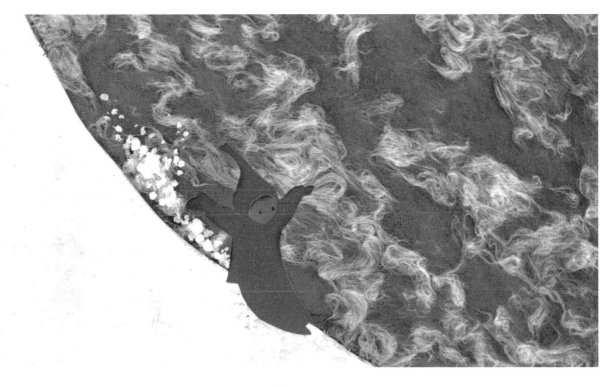

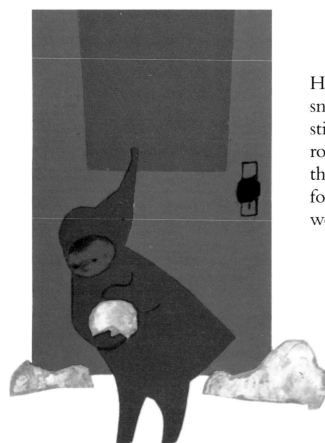

He picked up a handful of snow – and another, and still another. He packed it round and firm and put the snowball in his pocket for tomorrow. Then he went into his warm house.

He told his mother all about his adventures while she took off his wet socks.

And he thought and thought and thought about them.

Before he got into bed he looked in his pocket. His pocket was empty. The snowball wasn't there. He felt very sad.

While he slept, he dreamed that the sun had melted all the snow away.

But when he woke up his dream was gone. The snow was still everywhere. New snow was falling!

After breakfast he called to his friend from across the hall, and they went out together into the deep, deep snow.

TWINKLE, TWINKLE, LITTLE STAR

Illustrated by Sarah Pooley

TWINKLE, twinkle, little star,
How I wonder what you are,
Up above the world so high,
Like a diamond in the sky.

Pat Hutchins
THE WIND BLEW

THE WIND blew.

It took the umbrella from Mr White
and quickly turned it inside out.

It snatched the balloon from little Priscilla
and swept it up to join the umbrella.

110

And not content, it took a hat,
and still not satisfied with that,

it whipped a kite into the air
and kept it spinning round up there.

It grabbed a shirt left out to dry
and tossed it upward to the sky.

It plucked a hanky from a nose
and up and up and up it rose.

It lifted the wig from the judge's head
and didn't drop it back. Instead

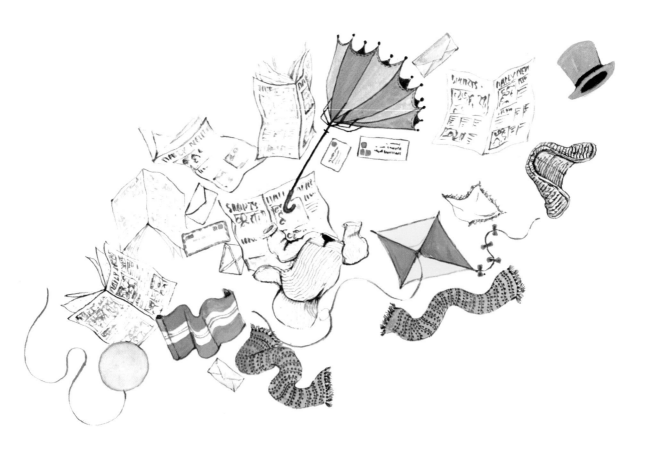

it whirled the postman's letters up,
as if it hadn't done enough.

It blew so hard it quickly stole
a striped flag fluttering on a pole.

It pulled the new scarves from the twins
and tossed them to the other things.

It sent the newspapers fluttering round,
then, tired of the things it found,

it mixed them up and threw them down

and blew away to sea.

I'M A LITTLE TEAPOT

Illustrated by Sarah Pooley

I'M a little teapot, short and stout;
Here's my handle, here's my spout.
When I see the tea-cups, hear me shout,
"Tip me up and pour me out."

Anthony Browne

WILLY AND HUGH

WILLY WAS lonely.

Everyone seemed to have friends. Everyone except Willy.

No one let him join in any games; they all said he was useless.

One day Willy was walking in the park …

minding his own business …

and Hugh Jape was running …

they met.

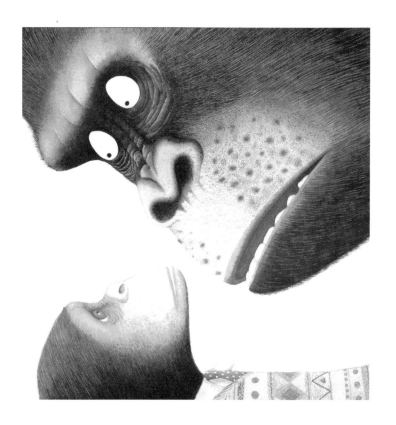

"Oh, I'm so sorry," said Hugh.
Willy was amazed. "But *I'm* sorry," he said, "I wasn't watching where I was going."
"No, it was *my* fault," said Hugh. "I wasn't looking where *I* was going. I'm sorry."
Hugh helped Willy to his feet.

They sat down on a bench and watched the joggers.
"Looks like they're *really* enjoying themselves," said Hugh.
Willy laughed.

Buster Nose appeared. "I've been looking for you, little wimp," he sneered.

Hugh stood up. "Can *I* be of any help?" he asked.
Buster left. Very quickly.

So Willy and Hugh
decided to go to the zoo.

Then they went
to the library,
and Willy read
to Hugh.

As they were leaving the library, Hugh stopped suddenly …

He'd seen a
TERRIFYING CREATURE …

"Can *I* be of any help?" asked Willy, and he carefully moved the spider out of the way.

Willy felt quite pleased with himself.
"Shall we meet up tomorrow?" asked Hugh.
"Yes, that would be great," said Willy.

121

And it was.

Grace Nichols
GRANNY GRANNY PLEASE COMB MY HAIR

GRANNY Granny
please comb my hair
you always take your time
you always take such care

You put me to sit on a cushion
between your knees
you rub a little coconut oil
parting gentle as a breeze

Mummy Mummy
she's always in a hurry – hurry
rush
she pulls my hair
sometimes she tugs

But Granny
you have all the time in the world
and when you're finished
you always turn my head and say
"Now who's a nice girl."

Susanna Gretz
IT'S YOUR TURN, ROGER!

IN ALL THE FLATS in Roger's
house it's nearly supper time.

"Roger, it's your turn to set the table."
That's his sister calling.

"I see you, Roger!"
That's his little brother.

"Roger, you know we all take turns at helping."
That's Roger's dad.

"Roger, it's *your turn*."
That's Roger's uncle.

"ROGER!
You heard what Uncle Tim said.
I don't want to hear another
word about it...

...and that's final!"
That's Roger's mum.

"OK, OK," moans Roger.

"In other families you don't have to help," Roger grumbles.
"Are you sure?" asks Uncle Tim. "Why don't you go and see?"

"All right, I *will*," says Roger.

He stomps out of the door…

…and on upstairs.
"Come in, come in," says the family
on the first floor.
"Do I have to set the table?" asks Roger.
"Certainly not, you're a guest. Come in
and have some fishmeal soup."

What a fancy supper table, thinks Roger…but what *horrible* soup!

"Excuse me," says Roger, and he hops upstairs.

"Come in, come in," says the
family on the second floor.
"Do I have to set the table?"
asks Roger.
"Certainly not, you're a guest.
Come in and have some
mud pancakes."

What a messy table, thinks Roger…and what *dreadful* pancakes!

No one notices as he slips out.

"Come in, come in," says the
family on the third floor.
"Do I have to set the table?"
asks Roger.
"Certainly not, you're a guest.
Come in and have a little snack."

This family doesn't even *have* a table…Roots and snails – YUK!

Roger hurries away.

"Come in, come in," says the family
in the top flat.
"Do I have to set the table?"
asks Roger.
"Certainly not, you're a guest.
Come in and have some milky
mush."
"Well…" says Roger.
He *is* getting
hungry.

Everyone in the top flat is busy
getting the supper table ready.

Roger sits by himself and watches.
If I weren't a "guest",
I could help too, he thinks.

131

"What's a guest?" he asks someone.
"Well…guests don't really live here."
"Oh," says Roger. "Now where *I* live…"

Just then a special smell creeps all
the way upstairs to the top flat.

"Where *I* live," shouts Roger, "there's
something *good* for supper

– and it's my turn to help!"

"I took your turn for you," says Uncle Tim.
"I'll take your turn tomorrow," says Roger, between mouthfuls.

Worm pie for dessert – whoopee! Roger's favourite.

Colin West
THE SILENT SHIP

I sailed a ship as white as snow,
As soft as clouds on high,
Tall was the mast, broad was the beam,
And safe and warm was I.

I stood astern my stately ship
And felt so grand and high,
To see the lesser ships give way
As I went gliding by.

Jeanne Willis
DR XARGLE'S BOOK OF EARTHLETS

Illustrated by Tony Ross

Gᴏᴏᴅ ᴍᴏʀɴɪɴɢ, class.

Today we are going to learn about Earthlets.

They come in four colours. Pink, brown, black or yellow … but not green.

They have one head and only two eyes, two short tentacles with pheelers on the end and two long tentacles called leggies.

They have square claws which they use to frighten off wild beasts known as Tibbles and Marmaduke.

Earthlets grow fur on their heads but not enough to keep them warm.

They must be wrapped in the hairdo of a sheep.

Very old Earthlings (or "Grannies") unravel the sheep and with two pointed sticks they make Earthlet wrappers in blue and white and pink.

Earthlets have no fangs
at birth.
For many days they
drink only milk through
a hole in their face.

When they have finished the milk they must be patted and squeezed to stop them exploding.

When they grow a fang, the parent Earthling takes the egg of a hen and mangles it with a prong.

Then she puts the eggmangle on a small spade and tips it into the Earthlet's mouth, nose and ears.

To stop them leaking, Earthlets must be pulled up by the back tentacles and folded in half.
Then they must be wrapped quickly in a fluffy triangle or sealed with paper and glue.

During the day,
Earthlets collect the
hairs of Tibbles and
Marmaduke, mud,
eggmangle and banana.

They are then placed in
plastic capsules with
warm water and a
yellow floating bird.

After soaking, Earthlets
must be dried carefully
to stop them shrinking.
Then they are sprinkled
with dust to stop them
sticking to things.

Earthlets can be
recognised by their
fierce cry,
"WAAAAAAA!"

To stop them doing this, the Earthling daddy picks them up and flings them into the atmosphere.

Then he tries to catch them.

If they still cry, the Earthling mummy pulls their pheelers one by one and says "This little piggy went to market" until the Earthlet makes a "hee hee" noise.

If they still cry, they are sent to a place called beddybyes.

This is a swinging box with a soft lining in which there lives a small bear called Teddy.

That is the end of today's lesson.

If you are all very good and quiet we are going to put our disguises on and visit planet Earth to see some real Earthlets.

The spaceship leaves in five minutes.

Colin West
GERALDINE GIRAFFE

THE longest
ever
woolly
scarf
was
worn
by
Geraldine
Giraffe.
Around
her
neck
the
scarf
she
wound,
but
still
it
trailed
upon
the
ground.

Jane Hissey
OLD BEAR

IT WASN'T ANYBODY'S BIRTHDAY, but Bramwell Brown had a feeling that today was going to be a special day. He was sitting thoughtfully on the windowsill with his friends Duck, Rabbit and Little Bear when he suddenly remembered that someone wasn't there who should be.

A very long time ago, he had seen his good friend Old Bear being packed away in a box. Then he was taken up a ladder, through a trap door and into the attic. The children were being too rough with him and he needed somewhere safe to go for a while.

"Has he been forgotten, do you think?" Bramwell asked his friends.

"I think he might have been," said Rabbit.

"Well," said Little Bear, "isn't it time he came back down with us? The children are older now and would look after him properly. Let's go and get him!"

"What a marvellous idea!" said Bramwell. "But how can we rescue him? It's a long way up to the attic and we haven't got a ladder."

"We could build a tower of bricks," suggested Little Bear.

Rabbit collected all the bricks and the others set about building the tower. It grew very tall, and Little Bear was just putting on the last brick when the tower began to wobble.

"Look out!" he cried as the whole thing came tumbling down.

"Never mind," said Bramwell, helping Little Bear to his feet. "We'll just have to think of something else."

"Let's try making *ourselves* into a tower," said Duck.

"Good idea!" said Bramwell.

Little Bear climbed on top of Rabbit's head and Rabbit hopped on to Duck's beak. They stretched up as far as they could, but then Duck opened his beak to say something, Rabbit wobbled, and they all collapsed on top of Bramwell.

"Sorry," said Duck, "perhaps that wasn't a very good idea."

"Not one of your best," replied Bramwell from somewhere underneath the heap.

"I know!" said Rabbit. "Let's try bouncing on the bed."

"Trust you to think of that," said Bramwell. "You never can resist a bit of bouncing, especially when it's not allowed."

Rabbit climbed on to the bed and began to bounce up and down. The others joined him. They bounced higher and higher but *still* they couldn't reach the trap door in the ceiling.

Duck began to cry. "Oh dear," he sobbed. "What are we going to do now? We'll never be able to rescue Old Bear and he'll be stuck up there getting lonelier and lonelier for ever and ever."

"We mustn't give up," said Bramwell firmly. "Come on, Little Bear, you're good at ideas."

But Little Bear had already noticed the plant in the corner of the room.

"I've got it!" he cried. "I could climb up this plant, swing from the leaves, kick the trap door open and jump in!"

In case it wobbled, Bramwell Brown, Duck and Rabbit steadied the pot. Little Bear bravely climbed up the plant until he reached the very top leaf. He took hold of it and started to swing to and fro, but he swung so hard that the leaf broke and he went crashing down. Luckily, Bramwell Brown was right underneath to catch him in his paws.

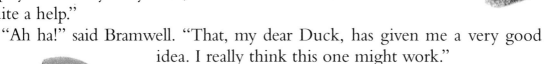

"That was a rotten idea," said Little Bear.

"What I was thinking," said Duck, "was that it is a pity I can't fly very well, as I could have been quite a help."

"Ah ha!" said Bramwell. "That, my dear Duck, has given me a very good idea. I really think this one might work."

In the corner of the playroom was a little wooden aeroplane with a propeller that went round and round.

"We could use this plane to get to the trap door," said Bramwell. "Rather dangerous, I know, but quite honestly I can't bear to think of Old Bear up there alone for a minute longer."

"I'll be pilot," said Rabbit, hopping up and down, making aeroplane noises.

"And I'll stand on the back and push the trap door open with my paintbrush," said Little Bear.

"But how will you get down?" asked Duck.

"I've already thought of that," said Bramwell, who hadn't really but quickly did. "They can use these handkerchiefs as parachutes and we'll catch them in a blanket."

Bramwell gave Little Bear two big handkerchiefs and a torch so he could see into the attic. Then he began to wind up the propeller of the plane. Rabbit and Little Bear climbed aboard and Bramwell began the countdown: "Five! Four! Three! Two! One! ZERO!"

They were off! The plane whizzed along the carpet and flew up into the air.

The little plane flew beautifully and the first time they passed the trap door Little Bear was able to push the lid open with his paintbrush. Then Rabbit

circled the plane again, this time very close to the hole. Little Bear grabbed the edge and with a mighty heave he pulled himself inside.

He got out his torch and looked around. The attic was very dark and quiet; full of boxes, old clothes and dust. He couldn't see Old Bear at all.

"Any bears in here?" he whispered, and stood still to listen.

From somewhere quite near he heard a muffled "Grrrrr," followed by, "Did somebody say something?" Little Bear moved a few things aside and there, propped up against a cardboard box and covered in dust, was Old Bear.

Little Bear jumped up and down with excitement. "Old Bear! Old Bear! I've found Old Bear!" he shouted.

"So you have," said Old Bear.

"Have you been lonely?" asked Little Bear.

"Quite lonely," said Old Bear. "But I've been asleep a lot of the time."

"Well," said Little Bear kindly, "would you like to come back to the playroom with us now?"

"That would be lovely," replied Old Bear. "But how will we get down?"

"Don't worry about that," said Little Bear, "Bramwell has thought of everything. He's given us these handkerchiefs to use as parachutes."

"Good old Bramwell," said the old teddy. "I'm glad he didn't forget me." Old Bear stood up and shook the dust out of his fur and Little Bear helped him into his parachute. They went over to the hole in the ceiling.

"Ready," shouted Rabbit.

"Steady," shouted Duck.

"GO!" shouted Bramwell Brown.

The two bears leapt bravely from the hole in the ceiling. Their handkerchief parachutes opened out and they floated gently down…landing safely in the blanket.

"Welcome home, Old Bear," said Bramwell Brown, patting his friend on the back.

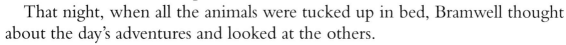

The others patted him too, just to make him feel at home. "It's nice to have you back," they said.

"It's nice to *be* back," replied Old Bear.

That night, when all the animals were tucked up in bed, Bramwell thought about the day's adventures and looked at the others.

Rabbit was dreaming exciting dreams about bouncing as high as an aeroplane.

Duck was dreaming that he could really fly and was rescuing bears from all sorts of high places.

Little Bear was dreaming of all the interesting things he had seen in the attic, and Old Bear was dreaming about the good times he would have now he was back with his friends.

"I *knew* it was going to be a special day," said Bramwell Brown to himself.

Christina Rossetti
WHAT IS PINK?

Illustrated by Millicent Sowerby

WHAT is pink? A rose is pink
By the fountain's brink.
What is red? A poppy's red
In its barley bed.
What is blue? The sky is blue
Where the clouds float through.
What is white? A swan is white
Sailing in the light.
What is yellow? Pears are yellow,
Rich and ripe and mellow.
What is green? The grass is green,
With small flowers between.
What is violet? Clouds are violet
In the summer twilight.
What is orange? Why, an orange,
Just an orange!

Dyan Sheldon

THE WHALES' SONG

Illustrated by Gary Blythe

LILLY'S GRANDMOTHER told her a story.

"Once upon a time," she said, "the ocean was filled with whales. They were as big as the hills. They were as peaceful as the moon. They were the most wondrous creatures you could ever imagine."

Lilly climbed on to her grandmother's lap.

"I used to sit at the end of the jetty and listen for whales," said Lilly's grandmother. "Sometimes I'd sit there all day and all night. Then all of a sudden I'd see them coming from miles away. They moved through the water as if they were dancing."

"But how did they know you were there, Grandma?" asked Lilly. "How would they find you?"

Lilly's grandmother smiled. "Oh, you had to bring them something special. A perfect shell. Or a beautiful stone. And if they liked you the whales would take your gift and give you something in return."

"What would they give you, Grandma?" asked Lilly. "What did you get from the whales?"

Lilly's grandmother sighed. "Once or twice," she whispered, "once or twice I heard them sing."

Lilly's uncle Frederick stomped into the room. "You're nothing but a daft old fool!" he snapped. "Whales were important for their meat, and for their bones, and for their blubber. If you have to tell Lilly something, then tell her something useful. Don't fill her head with nonsense. Singing whales indeed!"

"There were whales here millions of years before there were ships, or cities, or even cavemen," continued Lilly's grandmother. "People used to say they were magical."

"People used to eat them and boil them down for oil!" grumbled Lilly's uncle Frederick. And he turned his back and stomped out to the garden.

Lilly dreamt about whales.

In her dreams she saw them, as large as mountains and bluer than the sky. In her dreams she heard them singing, their voices like the wind. In her dreams they leapt from the water and called her name.

Next morning Lilly went down to the ocean. She went where no one fished or swam or sailed their boats. She walked to the end of the old jetty, the water was empty and still. Out of her pocket she took a yellow flower and dropped it in the water.

"This is for you," she called into the air.

Lilly sat at the end of the jetty and waited.

She waited all morning and all afternoon.

Then, as dusk began to fall, Uncle Frederick came down the hill after her. "Enough of this foolishness," he said. "Come on home. I'll not have you dreaming your life away."

That night, Lilly awoke suddenly.

The room was bright with moonlight. She sat up and listened. The house was quiet. Lilly climbed out of bed and went to the window. She could hear something in the distance, on the far side of the hill.

She raced outside and down to the shore. Her heart was pounding as she reached the sea.

There, enormous in the ocean, were the whales.

They leapt and jumped and spun across the moon.

Their singing filled up the night.

Lilly saw her yellow flower dancing on the spray.

Minutes passed, or maybe hours. Suddenly Lilly felt the breeze rustle her nightdress and the cold nip at her toes. She shivered and rubbed her eyes. Then it seemed the ocean was still again and the night black and silent.

Lilly thought she must have been dreaming. She stood up and turned for home. Then from far, far away, on the breath of the wind she heard,

"Lilly!
Lilly!"

The whales were calling her name.

Nicholas Allan

JESUS' CHRISTMAS PARTY

THERE WAS NOTHING the innkeeper liked more than a good night's sleep.

But that night there was a knock at the door.

"No room," said the innkeeper.

"But we're tired and have travelled through night and day."

"There's only the stable round the back. Here's two blankets. Sign the register."
So they signed it: "Mary and Joseph."

Then he
shut the door,
climbed the stairs, got
into bed, and went to sleep.

But then, later, there was
another knock at the door.

"Excuse me. I wonder if you could lend us another, smaller blanket?"

"There. One smaller blanket," said the innkeeper.

Then he shut the door, climbed the stairs,
got into bed, and went to sleep.

But then a bright light woke him up.
"That's **all** I need," said the innkeeper.

Then he shut the door, climbed the stairs, drew
the curtains, got into bed, and went to sleep.

But then there was **another** knock at the door.

"We are three shepherds."
"Well, what's the matter? Lost your sheep?"
"We've come to see Mary and Joseph."
"ROUND THE BACK,"
said the innkeeper.

Then he shut the door,
climbed the stairs,
got into bed,
and went to sleep.

But then there was yet **another** knock at the door.

"We are three kings. We've come – "

"ROUND THE BACK!"

He slammed the door, climbed the stairs, got into bed,
and went to sleep.

But *then* a chorus of singing woke him up.

"RIGHT – THAT DOES IT!"

So he got out of bed,

stomped down the stairs,

threw open the door,

went round the back,

stormed into the stable, and was just about to speak when –

"S s s h h !" whispered everybody,

176

"you'll wake the baby!"

"**Baby?**" said the innkeeper.

"Yes, a baby has this night been born."

"Oh?" said the innkeeper, looking crossly into the manger.

And just at that moment, suddenly, amazingly, his anger seemed to fly away.

"Oh," said the innkeeper, "isn't he **lovely!**"

In fact, he thought he was so special, he woke up **all** the guests at the inn, so that they could come and have a look at the baby too.

So no one got much sleep that night!

Ann and Reg Cartwright
THE WINTER HEDGEHOG

ONE COLD, MISTY AUTUMN AFTERNOON, the hedgehogs gathered in a wood. They were searching the undergrowth for leaves for their nests, preparing for the long sleep of winter.

All, that is, except one.

The smallest hedgehog had overheard two foxes talking about winter. "What is winter?" he had asked his mother.

"Winter comes when we are asleep," she had replied. "It can be beautiful, but it can also be dangerous, cruel and very, very cold. It's not for the likes of us. Now go to sleep."

But the smallest hedgehog couldn't sleep. As evening fell he slipped away to look for winter. When hedgehogs are determined they can move very swiftly, and soon the little hedgehog was far from home. An owl swooped down from high in a tree.

"Hurry home," he called. "It's time for your long sleep." But on and on went the smallest hedgehog until the sky turned dark and the trees were nothing but shadows.

The next morning, the hedgehog awoke to find the countryside covered in fog. "Who goes there?" called a voice, and a large rabbit emerged from the mist; amazed to see a hedgehog about with winter coming on.

"I'm looking for winter," replied the hedgehog. "Can you tell me where it is?"

"Hurry home," said the rabbit. "Winter is on its way and it's no time for hedgehogs."

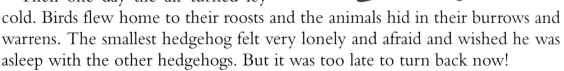

But the smallest hedgehog wouldn't listen. He was determined to find winter.

Days passed. The little hedgehog found plenty of slugs and insects to eat, but he couldn't find winter anywhere.

Then one day the air turned icy cold. Birds flew home to their roosts and the animals hid in their burrows and warrens. The smallest hedgehog felt very lonely and afraid and wished he was asleep with the other hedgehogs. But it was too late to turn back now!

That night winter came. A frosty wind swept through the grass and blew the last straggling leaves from the trees. In the morning the whole countryside was covered in a carpet of snow.

"Winter!" cried the smallest hedgehog. "I've found it at last." And all the birds flew down from the trees to join him.

The trees were completely bare and the snow sparkled on the grass. The little hedgehog went to the river to drink, but it was frozen. He shivered, shook his prickles and stepped on to the ice. His feet began to slide and the faster he scurried, the faster he sped across it. "Winter is wonderful," he cried. At first he did not see the fox, like a dark shadow, slinking towards him.

"Hello! Come and join me," he called as the fox reached the riverbank. But the fox only heard the rumble of his empty belly. With one leap he pounced on to the ice. When the little hedgehog saw his sly yellow eyes he understood what the fox was about. But every time he tried to run away he slipped on the ice. He curled into a ball and spiked his prickles.

"Ouch!" cried the fox. The sharp prickles stabbed his paws and he reeled towards the centre of the river where he disappeared beneath the thin ice.

"That was close," the smallest hedgehog cried to himself. "Winter is beautiful, but it is also cruel, dangerous and very, very cold."

Winter was everywhere: in the

air, in the trees, on the ground and in the hedgerows. Colder and colder it grew until the snow froze under the hedgehog's feet. Then the snow came again and a cruel north wind picked it up and whipped it into a blizzard. The night fell as black as ink and he lost his way. "Winter is dangerous and cruel and very, very cold," moaned the little hedgehog.

Luck saved him. A hare scurrying home gave him shelter in his burrow. By morning the snow was still falling, but gently now, covering everything it touched in a soft white blanket.

The smallest hedgehog was enchanted as he watched the pattern his paws made. Reaching the top of a hill, he rolled into a ball and spun over and over, turning himself into a great white snowball as he went. Down and down he rolled until he reached the feet of two children building a snowman.

"Hey, look at this," said the little girl; "a perfect head for our snowman."

"I'm a hedgehog," he cried. But no one heard his tiny hedgehog voice.

The girl placed the hedgehog snowball on the snowman's body and the boy used a carrot for a nose and pebbles for the eyes. "Let me out," shouted the hedgehog. But the children just stood back and admired their work before going home for lunch.

When the children had gone, the cold and hungry hedgehog nibbled at the carrot nose. As he munched the sun came out and the snow began to melt. He blinked in the bright sunlight, tumbled down the snowman's body and was free.

Time went on. The hedgehog saw the world in its winter cloak. He saw

bright red berries disappear from the hedgerows as the birds collected them for their winter larders. And he watched children speed down the hill on their sleighs.

The winter passed. One day the air grew warmer and the river began to flow again. A stoat, who had

changed his coat to winter white, changed it back to brown. Then the little hedgehog found crocuses and snowdrops beneath the trees and he knew it was time to go home. Slowly he made his way back to the wood.

From out of every log, sleepy hedgehogs were emerging from their long sleep.

"Where have you been?" they called to the smallest hedgehog.

"I found winter," he replied.

"And what was it like?" asked his mother.

"It was wonderful and beautiful, but it was also..."

"Dangerous, cruel and very, very cold," finished his mother.

But she was answered by a yawn, a sigh and a snore and the smallest hedgehog was fast asleep.

Vyanne Samuels

CARRY GO BRING COME

Illustrated by Jennifer Northway

IT WAS SATURDAY MORNING at Leon's house. It was a big Saturday morning at Leon's house. It was Marcia's wedding day. Marcia was Leon's sister.

Everyone in the house was getting ready for the big Saturday morning. Everyone was getting ready for the big wedding.

Everyone that was except Leon, who was fast asleep downstairs.

"Wake up, Leon!" shouted his mother upstairs.

But Leon did not move.

"Wake up, Leon!" shouted his sister Marlene upstairs.

But Leon did not move.

Leon's mother and his sisters, Marlene and Marcia, were so busy taking big blue rollers out of their hair, that they forgot to shout at Leon to wake up again.

They were getting ready for the big day.

They were getting ready for Marcia's wedding.

"Wake up, Leon," said Grandma softly downstairs.

Leon's two eyes opened up immediately.

Leon was awake.

"Carry this up to your mother," said Grandma, handing him a pink silk flower.

Leon ran upstairs to the bedroom with the pink silk flower. But before he could knock on the door, his sister Marcia called to him:

"Wait a little," she said, and she handed him a white head-dress. "Carry this down to Grandma."

So, Leon put the flower between his teeth, head-dress in his two hands, and ran down the stairs to Grandma.

When he got to his grandma's door, she called to him before he could knock.

"Wait a little," she said. He waited.

"Carry these up to Marlene," she said, and she poked a pair of blue shoes out at him.

So, Leon put the head-dress on his head, kept the flower between his teeth and carried the shoes in his two hands.

He tripped upstairs to Marlene.

But when he got to the bedroom door, Marlene called to him before he could knock.

"Wait a little," she said, and she poked a pair of yellow gloves through the door. "Carry these down to Grandma."

So, Leon put the gloves on his hands, the shoes on his feet, the head-dress on his head and the pink silk flower between his teeth.

He wobbled downstairs

to Grandma, who called to him before he could knock.

"Wait a little," she said. He waited.

"Carry this to Marcia," she said, and she poked a green bottle of perfume through the door.

"Mind how you go," she said.

So, Leon climbed the stairs holding carefully the green bottle of perfume, wearing carefully the yellow gloves, dragging carefully the blue shoes, balancing carefully the white head-dress, biting carefully the pink silk flower…when suddenly he could go no further and shouted:

"HELP!" from the middle of the stairs.

He nearly swallowed the flower.

His mother ran out of the room upstairs, his sister Marlene ran out of the room upstairs and Grandma rushed out of her room downstairs. There was a big silence. They all looked at Leon.

"Look 'pon his feet!" said his mother.

"Look 'pon his fingers and his hands!" said Marlene.

"Look 'pon his head!" said Grandma.

"Look 'pon his mouth!" said Marcia.

And they all let go a big laugh!

Leon looked like a bride!

One by one, Mother, Marcia, Marlene and Grandma took away the pink silk flower, the white head-dress, the green bottle of perfume, the blue shoes and the yellow gloves.

"When am I going to get dressed for the wedding?" asked Leon, wearing just his pyjamas now.

"Just wait a little!" said Grandma.

Leon's two eyes opened wide.

"YOU MEAN I HAVE TO WAIT A LITTLE!" he shrieked.

And before anyone could answer, he ran downstairs…and jumped straight back into his bed, without waiting even a little.

William Steig
DOCTOR DE SOTO

Doctor De Soto, the dentist, did very good work, so he had no end of patients. Those close to his own size – moles, chipmunks, et cetera – sat in the regular dentist's chair.

Larger animals sat on the floor, while Doctor De Soto stood on a ladder.

For extra-large animals, he had a special room. There Doctor De Soto was hoisted up to the patient's mouth by his assistant, who also happened to be his wife.

Doctor De Soto was especially popular with the big animals. He was able to work inside their mouths, wearing galoshes to keep his feet dry; and his fingers were so delicate, and his drill so dainty, they could hardly feel any pain.

Being a mouse, he refused to treat animals dangerous to mice, and it said so on his sign. When the doorbell rang, he and his wife would look out the window. They wouldn't admit even the most timid-looking cat.

One day, when they looked out, they saw a well-dressed fox with a flannel bandage around his jaw.

"I cannot treat you, sir!" Doctor De Soto shouted. "Sir! Haven't you read my sign?"

"Please!" the fox wailed. "Have mercy, I'm suffering!" And he wept so bitterly it was pitiful to see.

"Just a moment," said Doctor De Soto. "That poor fox," he whispered to his wife. "What shall we do?"

"Let's risk it," said Mrs De Soto. She pressed the buzzer and let the fox in.

He was up the stairs in a flash. "Bless your little hearts," he cried, falling to his knees. "I beg you, *do* something! My tooth is killing me."

"Sit on the floor, sir," said Doctor De Soto, "and remove the bandage, please."

Doctor De Soto climbed up the ladder and bravely entered the fox's mouth. "Ooo-wow!" he gasped. The fox had a rotten bicuspid and unusually bad breath.

"This tooth will have to come out," Doctor De Soto announced. "But we can make you a new one."

"Just stop the pain," whimpered the fox, wiping some tears away.

Despite his misery, he realised he had a tasty little morsel in his mouth, and his jaw began to quiver. "Keep open!" yelled Doctor De Soto.

"Wide open!" yelled his wife.

"I'm giving you gas now," said Doctor De Soto. "You won't feel a thing when I yank that tooth."

Soon the fox was in dreamland. "M-m-m, yummy," he mumbled. "How I love them raw...with just a pinch of salt, and a...dry...white wine."

They could guess what he was dreaming about. Mrs De Soto handed her husband a pole to keep the fox's mouth open.

Doctor De Soto fastened his extractor to the bad tooth. Then he and his wife began turning the winch. Finally, with a sucking sound, the tooth popped out and hung swaying in the air.

"I'm bleeding!" the fox yelped when he came to.

Doctor De Soto ran up the ladder and stuffed some gauze in the hole. "The worst is over," he said. "I'll have your new tooth ready tomorrow. Be here at eleven sharp."

The fox, still woozy, said goodbye and left. On his way home, he wondered if it would be shabby of him to eat the De Sotos when the job was done.

After office hours, Mrs De Soto moulded a tooth of pure gold and polished it. "Raw with salt, indeed," muttered Doctor De Soto. "How foolish to trust a fox!"

"He didn't know what he was saying," said Mrs De Soto. "Why should he harm us? We're helping him."

"Because he's a fox!" said Doctor

De Soto. "They're wicked, wicked creatures."

That night the De Sotos lay awake worrying. "Should we let him in tomorrow?" Mrs De Soto wondered.

"Once I start a job," said the dentist firmly, "I finish it. My father was the same way."

"But we must do something to protect ourselves," said his wife. They talked and talked until they formed a plan. "I think it will work," said Doctor De Soto. A minute later he was snoring.

The next morning, promptly at eleven, a very cheerful fox turned up. He was feeling not a particle of pain.

When Doctor De Soto got into his mouth, he snapped it shut for a moment, then opened wide and laughed. "Just a joke!" he chortled.

"Be serious," said the dentist sharply. "We have work to do." His wife was lugging the heavy tooth up the ladder.

"Oh, I love it!" exclaimed the fox. "It's just beautiful."

Doctor De Soto set the gold tooth in its socket and hooked it up to the teeth on both sides.

The fox caressed the new tooth with his tongue. "My, it feels good," he thought. "I really shouldn't eat them. On the other hand, how can I resist?"

"We're not finished," said Doctor De Soto, holding up a large jug. "I have here a remarkable preparation developed only recently

by my wife and me. With just one application, you can be rid of toothaches forever. How would you like to be the first one to receive this unique treatment?"

"I certainly would!" the fox declared. "I'd be honoured." He hated any kind of personal pain.

"You will never have to see us again," said Doctor De Soto.

"*No one* will see you again," said the fox to himself. He had definitely made up his mind to eat them – with the help of his brand-new tooth.

Doctor De Soto stepped into the fox's mouth with a bucket of secret formula and proceeded to paint each tooth. He hummed as he worked. Mrs De Soto stood by on the ladder, pointing out spots he had missed. The fox looked very happy.

When the dentist was done, he stepped out. "Now close your jaws tight," he said, "and keep them closed for a full minute." The fox did as he was told. Then he tried to open his mouth – but his teeth were stuck together!

"Ah, excuse me, I should have mentioned," said Doctor De Soto, "you won't be able to open your mouth for a day or two. The secret formula must first permeate the dentine. But don't worry. No pain ever again!"

The fox was stunned. He stared at Doctor De Soto, then at his wife. They smiled, and waited. All he could do was say, "Frank oo berry mush" through his clenched teeth, and get up and leave. He tried to do so with dignity.

Then he stumbled down the stairs in a daze.

Doctor De Soto and his assistant had outfoxed the fox. They kissed each other and took the rest of the day off.

Hans Christian Andersen, retold by James Riordan
THUMBELINA

Illustrated by Wayne Anderson

ONCE UPON A TIME there was an old widow who wished to have a child of her own. So she went to the wise woman of the village saying, "How I long for a little child. Can you help me?"

"Maybe I can, and maybe I cannot," replied the sage. "Take this magic barleycorn and plant it in a flowerpot. Then you shall see what you shall see."

"Thank you," said the widow, handing her a silver coin before hurrying home with the seed.

No sooner had she planted it than a tulip began to grow and bloom before her very eyes.

"What a pretty flower," she cried, kissing the petals. At once the tulip burst open with a pop. And in the very centre of the flower sat a teeny tiny girl, neat and fair, and no bigger than the woman's thumb. So she called her Thumbelina.

The widow made a bed from a varnished walnut shell, a mattress out of violet leaves: and sheets from the petals of a rose. Here Thumbelina slept at night. In the daytime she played upon the table top. Sometimes she would

row a little boat from one side of the lake to the other. Her boat was, in truth, a tulip leaf; her oars, two stiff white horse's hairs; the lake, a bowl of water ringed with daisies.

One night, however, while she lay sleeping in her cosy bed, a toad entered the room through a broken windowpane. It was big, wet and ugly, and it hopped upon the table where Thumbelina slept beneath her rose-petal sheet. When it saw the little child it croaked, "Here is the very wife for my son!"

Thereupon, it seized the walnut bed and hopped with it through the broken window and down into the garden.

Now, at the bottom of the garden flowed a stream; it was here, amidst the mud and the slime, that the toad lived with her son. And that son was more loathsome than his mother.

"Croak, croak, cro-o-ak," was all he said when he saw the little maid.

"Hush, you'll wake her," said the mother. "We won't be able to catch her if she runs away, she's as light as dandelion fluff. I'll put her on a water-lily leaf and that way she'll be safe while we make your home ready for the wedding."

Out in the stream grew a host of water lilies, their broad green leaves floating on the water. The mother toad set Thumbelina down on the leaf farthest from the bank. When the poor girl awoke the next day she found herself stranded and began to cry. There was no way she could reach the safety of the bank.

The little fishes in the water now popped up their heads to peer at the tiny maid. When they saw how sad she was, they decided to help her escape. Crowding about the leaf's green stalk, they nibbled on the stem until the leaf broke free. Slowly it drifted down the stream, bearing Thumbelina to safety.

On and on sailed the leaf, taking Thumbelina on a journey she knew not where.

For a time a dainty butterfly hovered overhead, then finally settled on the leaf. Thumbelina was so glad to have company that she took the ribbon from her waist and tied one end to the butterfly and one to the leaf. Now her boat fairly raced across the water, on and on and on.

But Thumbelina's happiness was not to last. Presently, a large mayfly swooped down, seized her in its claws and flew up into a nearby tree. How frightened was poor Thumbelina as she soared through the air.

The mayfly set Thumbelina down upon the largest leaf, brought her honey from the flower pollen and sang her praises to the skies, even though she was nothing like a mayfly. By and by, all the mayflies that dwelt within the tree came to stare at the tiny girl. Two lady mayflies waggled their feelers in

disgust, muttering scornfully, "But she has neither *wings* nor *feelers*. How ugly she is."

The mayfly who had captured Thumbelina began to have his doubts;

perhaps she really was as ugly as they said. Finally he made up his mind. He picked her up, carried her down to a daisy on the greenwood floor and left her there alone.

All through the summertime Thumbelina lived alone in the big wide wood. She wove herself a gossamer bed and hung it beneath a broad dock leaf, to shelter her from the rain. She ate honey from the flowers and drank dew each morning from their leaves.

Summer and autumn passed, and cold winter began its long reign. The birds that sang so sweetly flew away and the trees and flowers shed their blooms. Her dock-leaf canopy withered to a yellow stalk.

Thumbelina began to tremble with the cold, for her clothes were now quite threadbare. She was so frail and slender, poor little mite, that she would surely freeze to death. Snow began to fall. Each fluffy flake that fell upon her head was like an avalanche.

Now, close by the wood lay a cornfield. The harvest had long been taken in, leaving dry stubble standing stiffly in the earth. To the tiny maid, the corn stalks were like a great forest. It was here that Thumbelina came in search of shelter. All of a sudden she stumbled upon a little house. It belonged to a fieldmouse who lived there, warm and snug and with a well-stocked larder. Like a little beggar girl, Thumbelina knocked timidly at the door. "Little mouse, little mouse, please let me in," she cried. "I've had nothing to eat for these past two days."

"You poor little thing," said the mouse. "Come into my warm house and dine with me."

The fieldmouse soon took a liking to the child. "Stay here through the winter," she said. "You can keep my home clean and tell me fairy stories; I do so love a good story."

One day the fieldmouse announced, "We're going to have a visitor; my neighbour is coming to tea. He is rather a splendid fellow, with a rich velvet coat and a house much grander than mine. He would make you a fine husband. His sight isn't good, poor thing, so you'll have to tell him your finest stories." The neighbour was a mole.

Thumbelina was not at all keen to wed a mole.

Next day the mole arrived, dressed in his fine black velvet coat. True, he was clever and learned, but he hated the light; he hated the sunshine and flowers, even though he had never seen them.

After tea, Thumbelina was called upon to read and to sing. She sang so beautifully that the mole fell in love with her at once.

Mole had recently dug a tunnel from the fieldmouse's house to his own, so that they could visit each other when they liked. "Don't be afraid of the dead bird lying in the passage," he said. "It has no sign of injury and has all its feathers and its beak. Goodness knows how it got into my tunnel. It must have died of cold."

The mole took up a piece of rotten wood to use as a torch and led them down the tunnel. Then he pushed his long nose up through the soil to make room for daylight.

There lay a swallow, its wings pressed close by its sides, its head and legs drawn beneath it as if sheltering from the cold. The poor thing was frozen stiff.

Thumbelina felt so sad, for she loved the birds that had sung sweetly to her all through the summer. But the mole merely kicked the bird, saying, "Serves it right for all its chattering. How awful to be born a bird." The fieldmouse agreed.

Thumbelina was silent. Yet when the mole and the mouse had turned their backs, she bent down and kissed the swallow's eyes. Perhaps it was you who sang so sweetly to me, she thought.

That night Thumbelina could not sleep for thinking of the poor dead bird. At last she got up and wove a cover out of straw, carried it down the long

dark passage and put it over the bird's still form. "Farewell, pretty bird," she said. She pressed her head against the swallow's breast and was startled by a faint sound. The bird's heart was beating! She pressed the straw closer about its breast and fetched her own blanket to cover its head.

Next night she stole down the passageway again and was overjoyed to find the bird much better, although still weak.

"You must stay here in your warm bed until you are strong," said Thumbelina. "I will care for you."

The bird stayed underground the winter through, Thumbelina never breathing a word to the mole or mouse.

When spring arrived, it was time for the swallow to bid farewell. The tiny girl made a hole for it through the tunnel roof. How bright it was when the sun shone in.

"Come with me," said the swallow. "Sit upon my back and I'll take you far away to safety in the green wood."

But Thumbelina thought the fieldmouse would be lonely without her, so she shook her head sighing, "I cannot."

"Farewell then, little Thumbelina," said the swallow as it soared into the spring sunshine. Sadly she watched him go.

Thumbelina was cast down. The corn would soon be so tall that the mouse's house would be hidden from the sun.

"You must spend your time preparing for your wedding," said the fieldmouse, for the mole had finally proposed. "You should sew your wedding dress, and make the linen for your household."

The mole hired four strong spiders to help spin the thread and all through the summer Thumbelina spun and wove and sewed.

Every evening the mole came by to visit his wife-to-be, but all he said was, "Drat the summer. Hurry on winter." (For the sun baked the soil hard and made it difficult to dig. And once summer had passed and autumn came they would be wed.)

With every passing day Thumbelina began to dislike the mole more and more; he was so dull and vain.

Autumn came and Thumbelina's wedding dress was ready. "Four weeks more and you'll be wed," said the fieldmouse.

Thumbelina wept. "I cannot marry the mole!" she cried.

"Nonsense!" said the mouse. "He'll make the perfect husband; his velvet coat is fit for a king; his house has many rooms and larders. You ought to think yourself lucky."

The wedding day arrived. Mole came to fetch his bride and take her to his deep-down house. She would never see the blue sky again, never feel the

sun's rays, nor smell the flowers she loved. One last time she went outside to say goodbye to the world. She lifted up her arms towards the sky and stepped into the light. The corn was cut, but amid the stubble grew a lonely poppy bloom. "Farewell," she murmured. "If you see the swallow, give him my regards." Suddenly she heard a familiar sound.

"Tweet, tweet, tweet."

Looking up she saw her friend. Thumbelina told him all; how she had to marry the mole and live forever in the deep dark earth. She wept as she spoke.

"Winter will soon be here," said the swallow, "and I must fly away. Come with me; sit tight upon my back and we'll fly to a land where the sun always shines and where flowers blossom all the year through. You saved my life when I lay frozen and near death. Now it is my turn to help you." Thumbelina climbed upon the swallow's back and up they soared, above forests and lakes and snowy mountains.

At last they reached the land where the sun's breath was warm. But still the swallow did not stop. On it flew until it came to a tree-fringed lake.

"Choose a flower growing down below," said the swallow, "and there I will leave you to make your home." Thumbelina clapped her tiny hands.

On the soft green grass below lay fallen pillars of stone, around which grew pale, pure lilies. The swallow set her down upon a leaf. Imagine the girl's surprise when she saw a young man sitting in the centre of the flower. He was just as tiny, just as neatly formed and dainty as herself; yet he was wearing a pair of wings. "How lovely he is," said Thumbelina to the swallow.

"In every flower there dwells a youth or maiden," said the bird. "Each one is the spirit of the flower."

The young man looked at Thumbelina and thought her the loveliest creature he had ever seen. Taking her hand, he asked her to be his bride. Now here was a better husband than the loathsome toad or the mole in the velvet coat. Thumbelina readily agreed.

Right at that moment there appeared from every flower a tiny boy or girl, each bearing a gift. But the best gift of all was a pair of wings to enable her to fly.

"You shall have a new name," said the flower spirit. "From now on we will call you Maya."

"Farewell then, Maya," sang the swallow as he took flight.

Soon he would start his journey north to Denmark. It was there he had a nest, above the window of a storyteller – Hans Christian Andersen by name – who wrote down the tale related here.

Michael Ratnett
JENNY'S BEAR

Illustrated by June Goulding

JENNY HAD HUNDREDS OF BEARS of all shapes and sizes, and she loved every one of them. But what she wanted most in all the world was to meet a real live bear.

"Mum," she said one morning, "if we made a nice, cosy sort of den in the shed, would a real bear come and live in it?"

"I shouldn't think so," replied Mum kindly. "There aren't any real bears about here."

"Not even if I wished very hard?" said Jenny.

"I'm afraid not," said Mum. "But we can make a den just for you and your toy bears, if you like."

The shed was in a terrible state.

"Phew," said Mum, "I've never seen such a muddle. It must be years since this place was last cleaned!"

"It's no wonder that there aren't any bears living around here if all the sheds are this messy," said Jenny seriously.

"No wonder at all," said Mum.

When the den was ready, Jenny settled her bears in so that if a real bear did come he would feel at home among his own kind.

"There," she said. "You look just right. Now, I've got to go in for lunch, so you'll have to keep watch for me, and if a bear does turn up, be sure to make him welcome."

All through lunch Jenny kept wishing for a real bear to be waiting for her back in the den.

And then she hurried out to the shed with a tray full of special things for the bear to eat.

But the den was just as she had left it. There was no sign of a real bear anywhere.

"Bother!" said Jenny.

But she set out her tea things and her books just the same, and then sat down to wait patiently.

Jenny and her bears waited, and waited and waited. And just when it seemed that nobody was ever coming, there was a knock at the door.

"Come in," said Jenny.

And in stepped the biggest, brownest, friendliest-looking bear she had ever seen!

"Hello," he said. "I hope you don't mind me popping in, but I've come all the way from the Wild North searching for somewhere to spend the coming winter, and this is by far the cosiest-looking place I've found."

"Of course I don't mind," said Jenny. "I made this den specially for bears, and I've been wishing for a bear all day."

Then Jenny sat the bear down, and told him to help himself to the food. He had buns, biscuits and jelly, which he thought was wonderfully wobbly. But he was not at all sure about the tea Jenny poured out for him.

"Hmm," he said. "This cup doesn't look very full. What sort of tea is it?"

"It's *pretend* tea," said Jenny.

"Oh, that's all right then," said the bear. "Pretend tea is the sort that bears like best."

And he drank it all up in one go. "Another cup please,"

211

he said, "but not so much sugar this time thank you."

Then Jenny showed the bear her books.

"Which one would you like first?" she asked. "The happy one or the sad one?"

"The sad one," said the bear. "As long as it's not too sad."

But it was too sad.

"Boohoo, boohoo," blubbered the bear. "Stop it. You're making me cry!" And big tears ran down his furry face.

So Jenny read the funny story to cheer him up.

"Ho ho ho!" roared the bear. "No more, no more. My sides are going to split!" And they both rolled around on the floor until the whole shed shook.

"That was fun," said the bear. "What shall we do now?"

"I've got this," said Jenny, holding up a small bottle.

"Bubble mixture!" said the bear. "However did you guess? All bears love blowing bubbles."

212

Outside Jenny and the bear blew hundreds of shimmering bubbles.

"You're very good at this," said Jenny.

"My whole family are champion bubble-blowers," said the bear. "My grandad once blew a bubble that was so big it took him right up into the air, and carried him hundreds of miles away."

"Wow!" said Jenny. "Did he ever get home again?"

"Oh yes," said the bear. "He wrapped himself in brown paper and posted himself back. He was a very clever bear."

By the end of the day, Jenny and the bear were the closest of friends. So she was very sad when he said that it was time for him to go.

"But you said you were going to stay the winter," she said.

"Yes," said the bear. "It's not winter yet though, and I've got lots of things to do first."

"You will come back, won't you?" said Jenny. "And bring your friends."

"I'll try," said the bear. "But remember to keep wishing."

Then he gave Jenny a special bear hug, and set off down the road. Jenny waved the bear out of sight, and went indoors for supper.

The next morning Jenny jumped out of bed, dressed quickly, and ran out to the shed.

But the den was empty. The big brown bear who liked stories and blowing bubbles was not there.

"What's the matter?" said Mum.

"My bear's gone," said Jenny.

"Cheer up," said Mum, "you know there wasn't really a bear, don't you?"

The weeks went by, and the weather got colder; but though there was still no sign of the bear, Jenny never forgot him.

"There *was* a bear," she said to herself. "And he will come back. I just have to keep wishing."

Then it was Christmas morning. When Jenny drew back the curtains and looked out of the window, she saw something magical in the snowy garden.

She tugged on her coat and boots, and ran out for a better look.

"A Snowbear!" she gasped.

And then she saw the huge prints in the snow.

She followed them all the way to the shed.

Everything was silent as she carefully pushed open the door...

"SURPRISE!" roared a chorus of growly voices, for the shed was crowded with bears - real bears of every shape and size. And right in the middle sat Jenny's bear!

"I said I'd come back," he said. "And this time I've brought the tea,

and there's plenty for everyone."

"What kind of tea?" laughed Jenny.

"Why pretend, of course," said the bear.

"Oh, good,' said Jenny. "That's the kind I like best!"

John Ryan

PUGWASH AND THE BURIED TREASURE

I T WAS A DARK AND STORMY NIGHT; a great gale blew and the *Black Pig* was tossed high and low by the mountainous waves which broke across the Caribbean Sea.

The pirates were all down below, clinging to their hammocks and feeling dreadfully sea-sick. All, that is, except for two…

Tom the cabin boy was up on deck at the wheel, fighting to keep the ship into the wind. And, strangely enough, Captain Pugwash was up there too… poring over a map of a treasure island. He knew they must be near the island, and although he was terrified of the storm, Pugwash was far too greedy to risk missing the treasure. Eagerly he scanned the waves, then suddenly a gust of wind snatched the map from his grasp and as he started after it a great wave caught him and swept him off his feet, tossing him over the side of the ship into the raging waves below.

Poor Captain Pugwash! He hated cold water and he was a very poor swimmer. And he knew that in a storm like this even Tom wouldn't be able to turn the ship back to save him.

By now the *Black Pig* was disappearing into the darkness and Pugwash felt that his last hour really had come. Then all of a sudden…his hand struck something hard. LAND! It wasn't dry land but it was at least firm. In the darkness the Captain could just see the outline of a tiny rocky island. Desperately he dragged himself up on to it, and a moment later…he fell into an exhausted sleep.

When the Captain awoke it was dawn. The terrible storm was over, the sea was dead calm. And there he sat, all alone on his little island. Or *was* he alone?

From close by, on the other side of the rock in fact, he heard a snore…then a loud SNORT. And he knew that snort all too well. He looked round, and yes…there to his horror and terror sat his worst and most dreaded enemy, the wickedest and most ferocious pirate on the seven seas, Cut-throat Jake! Then Pugwash got another surprise…Cut-throat Jake was smiling!

At first of course the Captain was absolutely *terrified* but oddly enough, Cut-throat Jake seemed friendly. He told Pugwash how he too had been swept away by the storm and cast up on the island.

And very soon the two pirates were chatting away just like old friends.

Pugwash even shared his last bit of sea-watery chocolate with his old enemy.

At least he *pretended* it was his last piece of chocolate, and Cut-throat Jake *pretended* that he believed him!

Then, far away on the horizon, they saw a ship. Both pirates were very excited. "Why, ain't that lucky now that we've become mates!" said Jake. "With the two of us it'll be easy to attract their attention! Take yer jacket off, me hand-some!"

Jake stood on the rock and Pugwash climbed on to his shoulders and waved his coat wildly.

And the ship seemed to be getting closer... and closer...and closer, although in the early morning light it was difficult to be absolutely sure.

Captain Pugwash was beginning to feel rather dizzy so finally both pirates stood hand in hand on their little island and shouted for all they were worth.

Soon the ship was so close that Cut-throat Jake roared with delight and gave a blood-thirsty chuckle. "Why," he growled, "it's me own ship the *Flyin' Dustman*, and me own shipmates come to save me. Ho, ho!"

"And me too?" asked Pugwash nervously.

"Save *you*?" roared Jake. "You didn't *believe* all that clap-trap about 'bygones be bygones' did 'ee? That was just to get 'ee to help me make 'em see us! Nay! It's *me* that's for savin' and *you* that's for maroonin' on this 'ere island, aharrh!"

By this time Jake's pirates had arrived in their long-boat. And a moment later Cut-throat Jake was being helped aboard.

"B-b-but you can't *leave* me here!" cried Pugwash.

"Why that I can and that I *will*, you old scallywag," replied Jake.

And he was gone, and very soon the *Flying Dustman* was receding into the distance.

"Come back! Come BACK! shouted Captain Pugwash. But Jake and his crew only laughed at him. And very soon the Captain couldn't even hear that.

As the hot mid-day sun rose overhead and Jake's ship disappeared over the eastern horizon, poor Captain Pugwash gave up all hope. In fact, he was so hopeless and downcast he never noticed that over the *western* horizon *another* ship had arrived.

It was the Captain's ship, the *Black Pig*!

Eagerly the pirates rushed to the side.

In next to no time Tom the cabin boy was on his way to the tiny island in the dinghy. "Well done, Tom lad!" cried Pugwash. "I might have known none of you would rest until you had found your gallant Captain!"

"Well, as a matter of fact," said Tom, "it wasn't *you* we were looking for. We found your map after the storm; it was caught in the rigging. And with the map we found the island. And as for the treasure, Cap'n, why…YOU'VE BEEN SITTING ON IT!"

And sure enough they found under the rocks and sand an ancient rusty chest, which was absolutely *stuffed* with treasure!

That night they all had a very merry party aboard the *Black Pig*. As the pirates played with the sparkling loot and counted it all up, Captain Pugwash told them *his* version of the story: how he had cleverly spotted the island in

the storm, dived into the raging sea, swam ashore and took possession of the island, defending it against Cut-throat Jake, and finally how he had driven off Jake and his entire villainous crew!

"I just don't know *what* you'd do without me," remarked Captain Pugwash later as Tom prepared his bath.

"Hm, I felt we did pretty well on our own," thought Tom, "but even so, it's good to have our Cap'n back again!"

Edward Lear
THE OWL AND THE PUSSY-CAT

THE Owl and the Pussy-Cat went to sea
   In a beautiful pea-green boat,
They took some honey, and plenty of money,
   Wrapped up in a five-pound note.
The Owl looked up to the stars above,
   And sang to a small guitar,
"O lovely Pussy! O Pussy, my love,
   "What a beautiful Pussy you are,
       "You are,
       "You are!
"What a beautiful Pussy you are!"

Pussy said to the Owl, "You elegant fowl!
   "How charmingly sweet you sing!
"O let us be married! too long we have tarried:
   "But what shall we do for a ring?"
They sailed away for a year and a day,
   To the land where the Bong-tree grows,
And there in a wood a Piggy-wig stood,

With a ring at the end of his nose,
    His nose,
    His nose,
With a ring at the end of his nose.

"Dear Pig, are you willing to sell for one shilling
"Your ring?" Said the Piggy, "I will."
So they took it away, and were married next day
    By the Turkey who lives on the hill.

They dined on mince, and slices of quince,
    Which they ate with a runcible spoon;
And hand in hand, on the edge of the sand,
    They danced by the light of the moon,
        The moon,
        The moon,
They danced by the light of the moon.

Maggie Glen
RUBY

R<small>UBY FELT DIFFERENT FROM OTHER BEARS</small> – sort of special.

Mrs Harris had been day-dreaming
when she made Ruby. She didn't notice that
she'd used the spotted material that was meant
for the toy leopards. She didn't watch
carefully when she sewed on the nose.

Ruby wasn't surprised when she
was chosen from the other bears, but
she didn't like being picked up
by her ear.

"OUCH, GET OFF!" she growled.

Ruby's paw was stamped with an "S"
and she was thrown into the air.

"YIPEE-E-E-E! 'S' IS FOR
SPECIAL," yelled Ruby.

Ruby flew across the factory and landed in a box full of bears.

"Hello," she said. "My name's Ruby and I'm special - see." She held up her paw.

"No silly," laughed a big bear. "'S' is for second - second best."

"We're mistakes," said the bear with rabbit ears. "When the box is full, we'll be thrown out."

Ruby's fur stood on end; she was horrified.

More bears joined them in the box. At last the machines stopped.

They listened to the workers as they chatted and hurried to catch the bus home. They heard the key turn in the lock. Then everything was quiet. One by one the bears fell asleep.

All except Ruby - Ruby was thinking. The only sound was the sound of the big bear snoring.

Hours passed. Suddenly Ruby shouted, "That's it!"

"What's it?" gasped the rabbit-eared bear who woke up with a fright.

"Zzzzzzzzzzzzzzzz-w-w-what's going on?" groaned the big bear, rubbing his sleepy eyes.

"That's *it*," said Ruby again. "We'll escape."

"ESCAPE!" they all shouted. And they jumped out of the box.

"Let's go!" said Ruby.

They looked for a way out.

They rattled the windows.

They pushed at the doors.

"There *is* no way out," cried a little bear. "We're trapped."

"This way," shouted Ruby, rushing into the cloakroom.

They found a broken air vent.

It was a very tight squeeze. They pushed and they pulled, they wriggled and they waggled, until they were all in the yard outside.

They ran silently, swiftly, through the night and into the day.

Some ran to the country, some to the town.

Some squeezed
through letterboxes.

Some slipped through
open windows.

Some hid in toy cupboards.

Some crept into bed with
lonely children. But Ruby…

…climbed into the window of the very best toy shop in town.

The other toys stared at Ruby.

"What's the 'S' for?" squealed the pigs.

"Special," said Ruby, proudly.

All the toys shrieked with laughter.

"Scruffy," said the smart-looking penguin.

"Soppy," said the chimpanzee.

"Stupid," giggled the mice.

"Very strange for a bear," they all agreed.

"Don't come next to me," said a prim doll.

"Wouldn't want to," said Ruby.

"Stand at the back," shouted the other toys.

They poked, they pulled, they prodded and they pinched. Ruby pushed back as hard as she could, but there were too many of them.

So Ruby spent all day at the back of shelf.

Then, just before closing time, a small girl came into the shop with her grandfather.

They searched and searched for something – something different, something special.

"That's the one," said the little girl.

"Yes, Susie," said Grandfather, "that one looks very special."

Ruby looked around her. "Can they see me? IT'S ME! They're pointing at me. WHOOPEE-E-E-E!"

"We'll have that one, please," said Grandfather.

The shopkeeper put Ruby on the counter.

She looked at the "S" on Ruby's paw.

"I'm sorry, sir," she said, "this one is a second. I'll fetch another."

"No thank you, that one is just perfect," said Grandfather. "It has character."

Character, thought Ruby, that sounds good.

"Shall I wrap it for you?" the shopkeeper asked.

"Not likely," growled Ruby. "Who wants to be shoved in a paper bag?"

"No thank you," said Susie. "I'll have her just as she is."

They all went out of the shop and down the street.

When they came to a yellow door they stopped.

"We're home, Spotty," said Susie.

"SPOTTY, WHAT A CHEEK!" muttered Ruby.

"It's got a growl," said Susie, and she and her grandfather laughed.

Susie took off her coat and scarf and sat Ruby on her lap.

Susie stared at Ruby and Ruby stared back.

Suddenly, Ruby saw a little silver "S" hanging on a chain round Susie's neck.

Hooray! thought Ruby. One of us – a special.

SNOW-WHITE

Illustrated by Angela Barrett

ONCE UPON A TIME there was a castle in a wild place. A king and queen lived there; they loved each other dearly, and were happy.

One day the queen sat by the window, stitching pearls on to cloth of gold. It was winter, and very cold, and presently it began to snow.

She opened the window to listen for the sound of the king's hunting horn. But as she leant out, she pricked herself with her needle, so that a drop of blood fell on to the snow. When she saw it, she wished in her heart, "O, that I had a child as red as blood, as white as snow, and as black as the wood of an ebony tree!"

And her wish came true, for in the course of time she had a daughter, the most beautiful baby girl that ever was seen. She was called Snow-white, for her skin was white as snow; also her lips were red as blood, and her hair as black as ebony. But, alas! The poor young queen died when she was born.

Then the king was distracted with grief and would have shut himself up in his wild kingdom, but – for the child's sake – after a year he married again. His new bride was very young, and very beautiful; everybody said she was the most beautiful lady in the whole world. Nobody told him that she had a proud heart and a greedy, jealous temper. Nobody mentioned that.

Now this queen had a magic mirror, which hung on her bedroom wall. Sometimes, when she was alone, she would unveil it and look at herself – this way, that way – and oh! she was superlatively beautiful. After that she would whisper into the glass, sweetly, pleasantly,

*"Mirror, mirror on the wall,
Who is the fairest of us all?"*
And a soft, magical voice always answered,
"You are the fairest of them all."
Then the proud queen was satisfied.

Snow-white lived in a different part of the castle. She had her nurse and her own cook. When she was old enough a governess came to instruct her, and an old gentleman to teach her music and dancing. Years passed, and she grew to be so kind, and gentle, and funny, and clever, that everybody loved her.

Only the king did not visit her as often as he should, because she reminded him too painfully of the dead queen, her mother, whom he still loved. As for her stepmother, she thought Snow-white a timid, poor-spirited child, not worth a second glance.

But one day, when the stepmother queen bent her beautiful head to the magic looking-glass, and asked as usual,

*"Mirror, mirror on the wall,
Who is the fairest of us all?"*
the mirror answered,

*"Queen, you are full fair, 'tis true,
But Snow-white fairer is than you."*

Then the queen was horribly shocked. Her beautiful face turned yellow with envy and rage, and from that moment she hated Snow-white with all her heart. She could get no different answer out of the mirror, and she knew that it spoke the truth.

The queen's wicked passions grew in her, until she had no peace, day or night. At last she sent for a certain huntsman who was discontented with the king's service. She said to him, "You must take that evil girl Snow-white into the forest and kill her, and bring me back her heart as a proof."

He looked at her and said, "What will you give me if I do it?"

So she handed him a purse full of gold.

Next day, when Snow-white went riding, the huntsman lay in wait for her, and he grabbed her pony by the bridle, and led her deep into the forest by secret paths no one could follow. Then he pulled out his knife. But the trembling maiden threw herself at his feet, weeping and pleading for mercy. And she was so lovely, and cried so piteously, that in the end he could not bear to hurt her; besides, he knew that wild beasts would devour her quickly enough, once night fell. He killed a young boar instead and cut out its heart, which he gave secretly to the queen as a token.

The king sent all his soldiers into the forest to look for Snow-white, but she was nowhere to be found. So everyone went into mourning for her, and many bitter tears were shed. Even the wicked queen dressed herself in black velvet, while she was exulting in her heart.

Now when the huntsman rode away, leaving Snow-white alone in the forest, she stared about her in terror; even the rustling of the trees made her heart beat pit-a-pat. So she started to run. And the wild beasts of the forest ran too, but for company, not to harm her; they pitied her as she fled, bruising her poor feet and scratching herself on the brambles that grew everywhere under the trees.

She ran on and on until she was utterly exhausted. She had reached a clearing in the forest; it was already evening, and one star shone in the patch of sky above the trees. There in front of her stood a little house, with a neat garden all round. She went up the path and knocked on the door. Nobody answered … Still nobody … But she was so tired that she could not help it, she had to go in to rest.

The door opened into a nice clean kitchen. There was a table spread with a cloth and laid for supper: seven little plates of bread and cheese she counted, and seven little cups of wine. She was so hungry and thirsty that she took just a mouthful of bread and cheese from each plate, so as not to finish a helping. From each cup she took a sip of wine.

In the next room she found seven little beds lined against the wall, each with a spotless white pillow and quilt. She was so tired that she lay down on one of them, and praying to God that He would look after her, she fell asleep.

Now this little house belonged to a family of dwarfs, who toiled all day in the gold mines, deep within the mountains.

When it was quite dark, they came home, and they noticed at once that somebody had called while they were out. So they struck flint and lit their seven candles, so that the room was a blaze of light.

First they saw that their suppers had been tasted, and next they found Snow-white, fast asleep in the little white bed. They crowded round her, lifting up their candles with cries of astonishment. "O goodness! O gracious!" they exclaimed. "What beautiful child is this?" and they were full of joy and excitement, though they were careful not to wake her.

Snow-white was very frightened next morning, when she went into the kitchen and saw seven little men sitting round the table. But they were polite

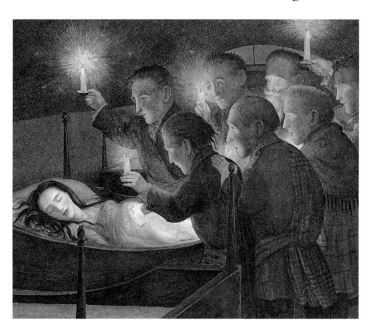

and friendly, and when she had told them her story, they said, "If you will keep house for us, cook and clean and wash and sew and knit, you may stay with us and we will look after you always."

"With all my heart," said Snow-white, and so the bargain was made. All day the seven dwarfs were away digging for gold in the mountain. When they came home, they found their supper ready, their clothes clean and mended, and the house neat as a new pin. So the weeks passed. But the good dwarfs never forgot to warn Snow-white, as they left the house each morning. "Beware of your stepmother, the wicked queen!" they said. "She will soon find you out. Take care, do not let anybody in!"

Now, the queen was sure that Snow-white was dead. But one day she drew back the veil from the magic looking-glass.

"*Mirror, mirror on the wall,*
Who is the fairest of us all?"

she asked with a smile. To her astonishment, the soft voice replied,

"*O Queen, thou art of beauty rare,*
But Snow-white, living in the glen
With the seven little men,
Is a thousand times more fair."

The queen turned white with fury, and her eyes glinted like a serpent's. She never doubted the mirror; she knew at once that the huntsman had deceived her, but he had gone where she could not get at him. So she disguised herself as an ugly old woman, and set off secretly to the house of the seven dwarfs.

The queen could not find her way through the forest; besides, the wild beasts would certainly have eaten her. So, instead, she had to walk a long and weary way, over seven mountains, until at last she came to the cottage. She limped up the path crying, "Collars and laces, belts and buttons! Pretty trifles for wives and maidens!"

Snow-white called from the window, "Good-day, Granny. What have you to sell?"

Then the old woman held up the silken laces which so pleased Snow-white that she said to herself, What harm can there be in this good old woman? So she unbarred the door, and the pedlar woman glided in.

"What a beautiful figure you have, my dear, to be sure!" she exclaimed. This was true, though she only pretended to admire it. "You shall have the laces as a present, only let me thread them for you."

And with quick fingers she threaded the coloured silks into Snow-white's bodice, in and out, all the way up. Then she pulled them so tight that the poor girl could not breathe and fell senseless to the ground. "So much for the fairest!" screeched the wicked queen, and she scuttled away in her old woman's shawl, like a spider.

The seven dwarfs, when they returned, were horrified to find Snow-white lying as dead on the floor. However, they noticed how tightly she was laced, and cut the bright silk at once, so that little by little she came back to life. Then she told them what had happened, and they cried out, "O dear child, you cannot see evil in anyone! The wicked queen has been here. You must be more careful, you must not let anybody in!"

As soon as the queen reached the castle, she hurried to her magic mirror, and demanded with a beating heart,

"Mirror, mirror on the wall,
Who is the fairest of us all?"

But the glass replied,

"O Queen, thou art of beauty rare,
But Snow-white, living in the glen
With the seven little men,
Is a thousand times more fair."

Then she knew her plan had failed, and her face became dark and hideous, reflecting the passions in her heart.

She had a little room, at the top of an empty tower, full of bats and spiders. Here she schemed, and poured, and scraped, and stirred, until she had brewed something very poisonous in her cauldron. Then she fetched a jewelled comb and steeped it in the brew, and when it was ready she wrapped it carefully in a cloth. She disguised herself once more, and set out for the cottage of the seven dwarfs. It was a long way over the seven mountains, but her envious heart drove her on.

When Snow-white heard her at the door, she looked out of the window. "You must go away," she said. "I cannot let anybody in."

But the evil woman held up the comb, so that the jewels in it caught the light most enticingly. Then she exclaimed, "Why, what beautiful hair you have! If you have been forbidden to let anybody in, then you must not. Only lean out of the window, and let me comb your beautiful hair."

Snow-white leant out of the window, so that her black hair hung down like a curtain of silk. But no sooner did the comb touch it, than its poison was released. The girl gave one cry and fainted dead away.

The poor little dwarfs were in a terrible fright when they discovered their beloved Snow-white, and, indeed, she would have died, only they came home earlier than expected. However, they soon found the comb and pulled it out of her hair, and then gradually the colour came back into her cheeks, and she opened her eyes. "O sweet child," they said, as they rubbed her cold hands and sponged her face with wine and water, "you must be

always on your guard. Your stepmother is evil and cunning, and she will stop at nothing to destroy you!"

The queen stood in front of her magic mirror.

"Mirror, mirror on the wall,
Who is the fairest of us all?"

But once more it answered,

"O Queen, thou art of beauty rare,
But Snow-white, living in the glen
With the seven little men,
Is a thousand times more fair."

The queen was now so furious, that she wanted to smash the glass with her clenched fists. Instead, she crept up to her secret room, and she toiled there many days. And at last she had prepared a poisonous apple, so deadly that she herself was almost afraid of it. She hid it in a basket of fruit, and herself in a third disguise. So she set off across the seven mountains, and that was a long, long way; but she sped on her wicked feet and by and by arrived at the cottage.

Snow-white heard the click of the gate and looked out. She could not see that this sunburnt peasant woman was the silver-haired granny with the laces, and the pedlar with the poisoned comb. She called out, "I am sorry, but I cannot let you in. The seven dwarfs have forbidden me to open the door!"

Still, she looked longingly at the fruit, all ripe and delicious in the woman's basket.

"Never mind, you are wise to be careful, and I shall take my fruit somewhere else. Bless you, pretty face! I shall leave you an apple, all the same," and she pretended to select the finest, and showed it to Snow-white, who shook her head at the window.

"Indeed, I cannot take it. I promised them I would not!"

"Are you afraid of poison? But I shall cut it, and eat half myself."

For the apple was made so that all the poison was in the red side. "The white for me, and you shall have the red!" cried the old woman, and took a bite from the white half and handed the rosy piece to Snow-white, who then could not resist biting into it. As soon as she tasted it, she shrieked and fell as if she had been stabbed to the heart. Then the wicked queen leered at her through the window, and cackled like a witch, "Well, well, my dear! I think you have done with being the fairest!"

As soon as she got home, the queen hastened to unveil her looking-glass.

*"Mirror, mirror, on the wall,
   Who is the fairest of us all?"*
Then at last came the reply,
   "You are fairest now of all."
So her jealous heart had peace – as much as a jealous heart can have.

The good little dwarfs came home at sunset. Once more they found their beloved Snow-white lying as dead upon the ground, but this time nothing they did could bring her back to life. They unlaced her, combed out her hair, washed her with water and wine – it was no use. Then they were full of grief, and prayed and lamented three bitter days, clustered round her bed in tears. After that, they would have buried her, except that they could not bear to put her into the ground; for her cheeks were still pink, as if she was sleeping and not dead.

So they made a glass coffin, and laid her in it, and wrote on it in letters of gold, "I am Snow-white, a king's daughter." Then they carried out the coffin, and arranged a place for it on the mountainside, and took it in turns so that one of them always watched over it. Three birds also came there to mourn for Snow-white – an owl, a raven, and a dove.

Snow-white lay in her glass coffin on the mountainside, and the days passed, the weeks and months passed, but she never changed – she was still as white as snow, as red as blood, and as black as ebony.

One day, it chanced that a prince rode that way who had been hunting in the forest. And when he looked in the coffin and saw Snow-white, he fell straightway in love with her. He gazed at her long and long, and at last he said to the dwarfs, "Let me have the coffin, and I will give you whatever you ask."

The dwarfs told him that they could not part with it for all the money in the world. But he begged more and more. "Dear dwarfs," he said, "I cannot live without this maiden. I beseech you to give her to me. I swear I shall honour you always, and look after you as if you were my brothers."

So at last they pitied him, and allowed him to take the coffin, and the prince told his servants to carry it away on their shoulders. But as they were taking it down the mountain, one of them stumbled, and the crumb of poison flew out of Snow-white's throat. She stirred, opened her eyes, and astonished at finding herself in a glass box, raised the lid and sat up, alive and well. Then the prince and the dwarfs were overcome with joy at the miracle, and the prince, falling at once to his knees, begged the beautiful girl to be his bride.

He took her to his father's castle, and the seven dwarfs he made his counsellors. A splendid feast was arranged, and wedding invitations were sent out all through the country. The stepmother queen received one; she did not know who the bride was. She put on her grandest clothes, and stood in front of her magic looking-glass for the last time, and said,

"Mirror, mirror on the wall,
Who is the fairest of us all?"
But the soft voice answered,
"O Queen, although you are of beauty rare,
The young bride is a thousand times more fair."

The queen then raged and swore, and bit her nails and vowed she would not go to the wedding. However, she did go, because there was no peace for her until she saw the bride. But she took with her a poisonous rose that she meant to leave on the young bride's pillow.

When she saw that it was Snow-white who was married, so happy and so beloved, the evil queen turned quite mad with jealousy, so that in her passion she clutched this deadly rose. Then she died miserably of her own poison.

But Snow-white and her prince, and the seven venerable counsellors, lived happily ever after.

Russell Hoban

HOW TOM BEAT CAPTAIN NAJORK AND HIS HIRED SPORTSMEN

Illustrated by Quentin Blake

Tom lived with his maiden aunt, Miss Fidget Wonkham-Strong. She wore an iron hat, and took no nonsense from anyone. Where she walked the flowers drooped, and when she sang the trees all shivered.

Tom liked to fool around. He fooled around with sticks and stones and crumpled paper, with mewses and passages and dustbins, with bent nails and broken glass and holes in fences.

He fooled around with mud, and stomped and squelched and slithered through it.

He fooled around on high-up things that shook and wobbled and teetered.

He fooled around with dropping things from bridges into rivers and fishing them out.

He fooled around with barrels in alleys.

When Aunt Fidget Wonkham-Strong asked him what he was doing, Tom said that he was fooling around.

"It looks very like playing to me," said Aunt Fidget Wonkham-Strong. "Too much playing is not good, and you play too much. You had better stop it and do something useful."

"All right," said Tom.

But he did not stop. He did a little fooling around with two or three cigar bands and a paper clip.

At dinner Aunt Fidget Wonkham-Strong, wearing her iron hat, said, "Eat your mutton and your cabbage-and-potato sog."

"All right," said Tom. He ate it.

After dinner Aunt Fidget Wonkham-Strong said, "Now learn off pages 65 to 76 of the Nautical Almanac, and that will teach you not to fool around so much."

"All right," said Tom.

He learned them off.

"From now on I shall keep an eye on you," Aunt Fidget Wonkham-Strong said, "and if you do not stop fooling around I shall send for Captain Najork and his hired sportsmen."

"Who is Captain Najork?" said Tom.

"Captain Najork," said Aunt Fidget Wonkham-Strong, "is seven feet tall, with eyes like fire, a voice like thunder, and a handlebar moustache. His trousers are always freshly pressed, his blazer is immaculate, his shoes are polished mirror-bright, and he is every inch a terror. When Captain Najork is sent for he comes up the river in his pedal boat, with his hired sportsmen

all pedalling hard. He teaches fooling-around boys the lesson they so badly need, and it is not one that they soon forget."

Aunt Fidget Wonkham-Strong kept an eye on Tom. He did not stop fooling around. He did low and muddy fooling around and he did high and wobbly fooling around. He fooled around with dropping things off bridges and he fooled around with barrels in alleys.

"Very well," said Aunt Fidget Wonkham-Strong at table in her iron hat. "Eat your greasy bloaters."

Tom ate them.

"I have warned you," said Aunt Fidget Wonkham-Strong, "that I should send for Captain Najork if you did not stop fooling around. I have done that. As you like to play so much, you shall play against Captain Najork and his hired sportsmen. They play hard games and they play them jolly hard. Prepare yourself."

"All right," said Tom. He fooled around with a bottle-top and a burnt match.

The next day Captain Najork came up the river with his hired sportsmen pedalling his pedal boat.

They came ashore smartly, carrying an immense brown-paper parcel. They marched into the garden, one, two, three, four. Captain Najork was only six feet tall. His eyes were not like fire, his voice was not like thunder.

"Right," said Captain Najork. "Where is the sportive infant?"

"There," said Aunt Fidget Wonkham-Strong.

"Here," said Tom.

"Right," said the Captain. "We shall play womble, muck, and sneedball, in that order." The hired sportsmen sniggered as they undid the immense brown-paper parcel, set up the womble run, the ladders and the net, and

251

distributed the rakes and stakes.

"How do you play womble?" said Tom.

"You'll find out," said Captain Najork.

"Who's on my side?" said Tom.

"Nobody," said Captain Najork. "Let's get started."

Womble turned out to be a shaky, high-up, wobbling and teetering sort of a game, and Tom was used to that kind of fooling around. The Captain's side raked first. Tom staked. The hired sportsmen played so hard that they wombled too fast, and were shaky with the rakes. Tom fooled around the way he always did, and all his stakes dropped true. When it was his turn to rake he did not let Captain Najork and the hired sportsmen score a single rung, and at the end of the snetch he won by six ladders.

"Right," said Captain Najork, clenching his teeth. "Muck next. Same sides."

The court was laid out at low tide in the river mud. Tom mucked first, and slithered through the marks while the hired sportsmen poled and shovelled. Tom had fooled around with mud so much that he scored time after time.

Captain Najork's men poled too hard and shovelled too fast and tired themselves out. Tom just mucked about and fooled around, and when the tide came in he led the opposition 673 to 49.

"Really," said Aunt Fidget Wonkham-Strong to Captain Najork, "you must make an effort to teach this boy a lesson."

"Some boys learn hard," said the Captain, chewing his moustache. "Now for sneedball."

The hired sportsmen brought out the ramp, the slide, the barrel, the bobble, the sneeding tongs, the bar, and the grapples. Tom saw at once that sneedball was like several kinds of fooling around that he was particularly good at. Partly it was like dropping things off bridges into rivers and fishing them out and partly it was like fooling around with barrels in alleys.

"I had better tell you," said the Captain to Tom, "that I played in the Sneedball Finals five years running."

"They couldn't have been very final if you had to keep doing it for five years," said Tom. He motioned the Captain aside, away from Aunt Fidget Wonkham-Strong. "Let's make this interesting," he said.

"What do you mean?" said the Captain.

"Let's play *for* something," said Tom. "Let's say if I win I get your pedal boat."

"What do I get if *I* win?" said the Captain. "Because I am certainly going to win *this* one."

"You can have Aunt Fidget Wonkham-Strong," said Tom.

"She's impressive," said the Captain. "I admit that freely. A very impressive lady."

"She fancies you," said Tom. "I can tell by the way she looks sideways at you from underneath her iron hat."

"No!" said the Captain.

"Yes," said Tom.

"And you'll part with her if she'll have me?" said the Captain.

"It's the only sporting thing to do," said Tom.

"Agreed then!" said the Captain. "By George! I'm almost sorry that I'm going to have to teach you a lesson by beating you at sneedball."

"Let's get started," said Tom.

The hired sportsmen had first slide. Captain Najork himself barrelled, and he and his men played like demons. But Tom tonged the bobble in the same fooling-around way that he fished things out of rivers, and he quickly moved into the lead. Captain Najork sweated big drops, and he slid his barrel too hard so it hit the stop and slopped over. But Tom just fooled around, and when it was his slide he never spilled a drop.

Darkness fell, but they shot up flares and went on playing. By three o'clock in the morning Tom had won by 85 to 10. As the last flare went up above the garden he looked down from the ramp at the defeated Captain and his hired sportsmen and he said, "Maybe that will teach you not to fool around with a boy who knows how to fool around."

Captain Najork broke down and wept, but Aunt Fidget Wonkham-Strong had him put to bed and brought him peppermint tea, and then he felt better.

Tom took his boat and pedalled to the next town down the river. There he advertised in the newspaper for a new aunt. When he found one that he liked, he told her, "No greasy bloaters, no mutton and no cabbage-and-potato sog. No Nautical Almanac. And I do lots of fooling around. Those are my conditions."

The new aunt's name was Bundlejoy Cosysweet. She had a floppy hat with flowers on it. She had long, long hair.

"That sounds fine to me," she said. "We'll have a go."

Aunt Fidget Wonkham-Strong married Captain Najork even though he had lost the sneedball game, and they were very happy together. She made the hired sportsmen learn off pages of the Nautical Almanac every night after dinner.

Virginia Mayo

DON'T FORGET ME, FATHER CHRISTMAS

IT WAS CHRISTMAS EVE. Through the night, the snow had gently fallen until it covered sleeping towns and villages where children lay good in their beds, waiting for Father Christmas. Close to midnight, most children were asleep, except for one: a baby who was wide awake and gazing thoughtfully up at the sky.

Meanwhile, in his sleigh, Father Christmas was tired. He'd been to every country with his great big sack - landed on rooftops, squeezed through chimney-pots, and struggled up and down chimneys until he had finally arrived at the last house.

Lizzie and Robert were fast asleep and never heard Father
Christmas as he tiptoed up to the beds as carefully as he could with
his bent back and aching feet. As he stuffed their stockings with toys,
he was already thinking of that lovely cup of tea waiting for him
back at the North Pole when he was finished.

He didn't notice a pair of eyes watching his every move from a
dark corner across the room. Neither did he spot
another red Christmas stocking dangling
over the side of the cot.

The baby clapped his hands together.
Oh at last . . . there he is! OI! Me next, Father Christmas!
But Father Christmas was off out the door and back on to the
roof.

 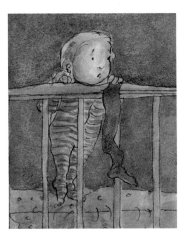 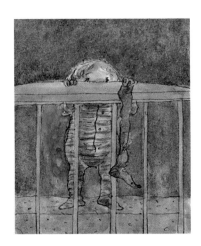

Just a minute . . . where are you going?

The baby was left quite alone. So he waited . . . and he waited.

It's all right. I'm sure he'll be back in a minute . . . He is COMING, isn't he? No! He can't . . . he can't have FORGOTTEN me! He HAS! He's forgotten me! I'm all alone, waiting with my stocking . . . and he's never going to come . . .

At first, the baby began to cry, then he sat up with a start, threw

his fat little bottom over the side of the cot and crawled off at speed, holding up his precious stocking tightly.

Well, I'm not giving up just like that!

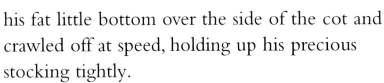

Up on the roof, the reindeer were surprised by the sight of a sooty baby's head appearing out of the chimney. "Good heavens!" cried a deer. "Did you see that?"

"Yes, I did," replied another. "Do you think he knows there's a baby on the roof ?"

Sadly, Father Christmas had his back to it all and had no idea that the furious baby was crying and pleading and shaking his fist at him.

"Reindeer away!" ordered Father
Christmas, climbing aboard the sleigh.
But the baby was not going to be stopped.
  Wait for me . . . !

He grabbed hold of the sleigh as it began to rise slowly in the air. Up and up he went, rising higher in the sky, holding tightly and never daring to look down far below as houses, cities, fields and oceans whizzed by. It was a good thing no one on the ground was watching.

Soon a small landing strip of lighted flares came into view in the middle of the snowy mountains of the North Pole. A crowd of elves had lined up outside Father Christmas's house to welcome him with a hot steaming cup of tea. As the reindeer were led away for a well-earned rest, one of the elves let out a cry: "Look at this!"

Everyone came running to see. "It's a baby!"

"Oh, Father Christmas, really! How could you? Didn't you know he was there?"

"But . . . but . . . how . . . ?" Father Christmas felt so silly he didn't know what to say. Then he saw the baby's stocking empty.

You FORGOT me!

The baby burst into tears.

"Right," said Father Christmas. "I know what we can do about that!'

So saying, he picked up the baby, dried his eyes and carried him to the workshop where the rest of the elves were packing and finishing off the last of the toys to be put away for next year.

By the time they reached the workshop, the news had reached the elves that silly old Father Christmas had brought a stowaway baby back on the sleigh.

"Let's give the baby something really special to take back," said the lady elves as they gathered soft toys into boxes.

The baby was thrilled when he saw the workshop. Every toy he could want was there, but the biggest and best of them was a large brown bear and that was what the baby chose.

Father Christmas put on his leather jacket and gave the baby his red hat and coat to wear to keep him warm on his journey home.

By the time they got back to the baby's bedroom he was asleep and Father Christmas gently laid him in his cot without waking him, and slipped quietly away.

At first light of Christmas morning, Lizzie and Robert were up and rummaging through their Christmas stockings, eating their sweets and throwing off wrapping paper. The baby was usually the first one to wake up and yet there he was, flat out in his cot and not a sound.

"Do you think he's all right?" asked Lizzie.

"He's lying very still," said Robert, "pull his covers off!"

"Wake up, sleepy, it's Christmas Day!"

But the baby was awake. Up he sat with a wink . . . and a big red fluffy thing on top of his head.

"What on earth is he wearing?" cried the children.

Father Christmas had forgotten his hat!

Peter Bowman
TINY TED'S BIG ADVENTURE

TINY TED woke up with a big yawn.
"Breakfast time," said Mouse.

"It's so quiet here," sighed
Tiny Ted.

"I wonder what it's
like out there."

"Phew, that was a
tight squeeze..."

"...Oh, what a lovely morning. I
think I'll have a little holiday."

"This is perfect!"

"I can go sailing..."

"...and sunbathing."

"But, maybe there isn't
room for two."

"Lucky I can swim.
Whoa, what's happening?"

"Oh thank you. I think I'm
safer on dry land."

"Phew, it's getting hot. I'll
shelter for a while in this cave."

"Whoops!"

"Mmm, this is nice and soft.
I'll just dry myself off."

"Oh, excuse me. I thought you
were a powder puff."

"Now I'm stuck, with no
one to rescue me."

"Thank you. Country people are very kind."

"But how do I get down?"

"By whirligig, of course! Whee!"

"Oh dear. No more sun."

"I think it's time to go home."

"But which way?"

"Oh, help. I'm lost and it's dark and I'm very, very small."

"There you are," said Mouse.
"I'm glad I've found you."

"So am I," said Tiny Ted.
"I've had a big adventure.
But really…"

"…there's no place like home."

THE END

Susan Varley
BADGER'S PARTING GIFTS

BADGER WAS DEPENDABLE, reliable, and always ready to lend a helping paw. He was also very old, and he knew almost everything. Badger was so old that he knew he must soon die.

Badger wasn't afraid of death. Dying meant only that he would leave his body behind and, as his body didn't work as well as it had in days gone by, Badger wasn't too concerned about that. His only worry was how his friends would feel when he was gone. Hoping to prepare them, Badger had told them that someday soon he would be going down the Long Tunnel, and he hoped they wouldn't be too sad when it happened.

One day, as Badger was watching Mole and Frog race down the hillside, he felt especially old and tired. He wished more than anything that he could run with them, but he knew his old legs wouldn't let him. He watched Mole and Frog for a long time, enjoying the sight of his friends having a good time.

It was late when he arrived home. He wished the moon good night and closed the curtains on the cold world outside. He made his way slowly down to the warm fire that was waiting for him deep underground.

He had his supper and then sat down at his desk to write a letter. When he had finished, he settled down in his rocking chair near the fire. He gently rocked himself to and fro and soon was fast asleep having a strange yet wonderful dream like none he'd ever had before.

Much to Badger's surprise, he was running. Ahead of him was a very long tunnel. His legs felt strong and sure as he ran towards it. He no longer needed his walking stick, so he left it lying on the floor of the tunnel. Badger moved swiftly, running faster and faster through the long passageway, until his paws no longer touched the earth. He felt himself turning head over paws, falling and tumbling, but nothing hurt. He felt free. It was as if he had fallen out of his body.

The following day Badger's friends gathered anxiously outside Badger's door. They were worried because he hadn't come out to say good morning as he always did.

Fox broke the sad news that Badger was dead and read Badger's note to them. It said simply, "Gone down the Long Tunnel. Bye bye, Badger."

All the animals had loved Badger, and everyone was very sad. Mole especially felt lost, alone and desperately unhappy.

In bed that night Mole could think only of Badger. Tears rolled down his velvety nose, soaking the blankets he clung to for comfort.

Outside, it began to snow. Winter had begun, and soon a thick layer of

snow hid the animals' homes, where they would stay snug and warm during the cold months.

The snow covered the countryside, but it didn't conceal the sadness that Badger's friends felt.

Badger had always been there when anyone needed him. The animals all wondered what they would do now that he was gone. Badger had told them not to be unhappy, but it was hard not to be.

As spring drew near, the animals often visited each other and talked about the days when Badger was alive.

Mole was good at using scissors, and he told about the time Badger had taught him how to cut out a chain of moles from a piece of folded paper. Paper moles had littered the ground that day. Mole remembered the joy he'd felt when he had finally succeeded in making a complete chain of moles with all the paws joined.

Frog was an excellent skater. He recalled how

Badger had helped him take his first slippery steps on the ice. Badger had gently guided him across the ice until he had gained enough confidence to glide out on his own.

Fox remembered how, when he was a young cub, he could never knot his tie properly until Badger showed him how.

"Starting with the wide end of the tie, it's right over left, once around to the back, up, then down through the crossover and, holding the back of the tie, push the knot up to the neck."

Fox could now tie every knot ever invented and some he'd made up himself. And of course his own necktie was always perfectly knotted.

Badger had given Mrs Rabbit his special recipe for gingerbread and had shown her how to bake gingerbread rabbits. Mrs Rabbit was well known throughout the countryside for her excellent cooking. As she talked

about her first cooking lesson with Badger, so long ago, she could almost smell the wonderful fragrance of gingerbread fresh from the oven.

Each of the animals had a special memory of Badger – something he had taught them that they could now do extremely well. He had given them each a parting gift to treasure always. Using these gifts they would be able to help each other.

As the last of the snow melted, so did the animals' sadness. Whenever Badger's name was mentioned, someone remembered another story that made them all smile.

One warm spring day as Mole was walking on the hillside where he'd last seen Badger, he wanted to thank his friend for his parting gift.

"Thank you, Badger," he said softly, believing that Badger would hear him.

And…somehow…Badger did.

Margaret Mahy
BUBBLE TROUBLE

Illustrated by Tony Ross

LITTLE Mabel blew a bubble and it caused a lot of
trouble...
Such a lot of bubble trouble in a bibble-bobble way.
For it broke away from Mabel as it bobbed across the
table,
Where it bobbled over Baby, and it wafted him away.

The baby didn't quibble. He began to smile and
dribble,
For he liked the wibble-wobble of the bubble in the
air.
But Mabel ran for cover as the bubble bobbed above
her,
And she shouted out for Mother who was putting up
her hair.

At the sudden cry of trouble, Mother took off at the
  double,
For the squealing left her reeling…made her
  terrified and tense,
Saw the bubble for a minute, with the baby bobbing
  in it,
As it bibbled by the letter-box and bobbed across the
  fence.

In her garden, Chrysta Gribble had begun to cry and
  cavil
At her lazy brother, Greville, reading novels in his
  bed.
But she bellowed, "Gracious, Greville!" and she
  grovelled on the gravel,
When the baby in the bubble bibble-bobbled
  overhead.

In a garden folly, Tybal, and his jolly mother, Sybil,
Sat and played a game of Scrabble, shouting shrilly as
  they scored.
But they both began to babble and to scrobble with
  the Scrabble
As the baby in the bubble bibble-bobbled by the
  board.

Then crippled Mr Copple and his wife (a crabby couple),
Set out arm in arm to hobble and to squabble down the lane.
But the baby in the bubble turned their hobble to a joggle
As they raced away like rockets…and they've never limped again.

Even feeble Mrs Threeble in a muddle with her needle
(Matching pink and purple patches for a pretty patchwork quilt),
When her older sister told her, tossed the quilt across her shoulder,
As she set off at a totter in her tattered tartan kilt.

At the shops a busy rabble met to gossip and to
    gabble,
Started gibbering and goggling as the bubble bobbled
    by.
Mother, hand in hand with Mabel, flew as fast as she
    was able,
Full of trouble lest the bubble burst or vanish in the sky.

After them came Greville Gribble in his nightshirt,
    with his novel
(All about a haunted hovel) held on high above his
    head,
Followed by his sister, Chrysta (though her boots had
    made a blister),
Then came Tybal, pulling Sybil, with the Scrabble for
    a sled.

After them the Copple couple came cavorting at the
    double,
Then a jogger (quite a slogger) joined the crowd who
    called and coughed.
Up above the puzzled people – up towards the chapel
    steeple –
Rose the bubble (with the baby) slowly lifting up
    aloft.

There was such a flum-a-diddle (Mabel huddled in
  the middle),
Canon Dapple left the chapel, followed by the chapel
  choir.
And the treble singer, Abel, threw an apple core at
  Mabel,
As the baby in the bubble bobbled up a little higher.

Oh, they giggled and they goggled until all their
  brains were boggled,
As the baby in the bubble rose above the little town.
"With the problem let us grapple," murmured kindly
  Canon Dapple,
"And the problem we must grapple with is bringing
  Baby down.

Now, let Mabel stand on Abel, who could stand in
  turn on Tybal,
Who could stand on Greville Gribble, who could
  stand upon the wall,
While the people from the shop'll stand to catch them
  if they topple,
Then perhaps they'll reach the bubble, saving Baby
  from a fall."

But Abel, though a treble, was a rascal and a rebel,
Fond of getting into trouble when he didn't have to
    sing.
Pushing quickly through the people, Abel clambered
    up the steeple
With nefarious intentions and a pebble in his sling!

Abel quietly aimed the pebble past the steeple of the
    chapel,
At the baby in the bubble wibble-wobbling way up
    there.
And the pebble *burst* the bubble! So the future seemed
    to fizzle
For the baby boy who grizzled as he tumbled through
    the air.

What a moment for a mother as her infant plunged
    above her!
There were groans and gasps and gargles from the
    horror-stricken crowd.
Sibyl said, "Upon my honour, *there's* a baby who's a
    goner!"
And Chrysta hissed with emphasis, "It shouldn't be
    allowed!"

But Mabel, Tybal, Greville, and the jogger
    (christened Neville)
Didn't quiver, didn't quaver, didn't drivel, shrivel,
    wilt.
But as one they made a swivel, and with action (firm
    but civil),
They divested Mrs Threeble of her pretty patchwork
    quilt.

Oh, what calculated catchwork! Baby bounced into
    the patchwork,
Where his grizzles turned to giggles and to wriggles of
    delight!
And the people stared dumbfounded, as he bobbled
    and rebounded,
Till the baby boy was grounded and his mother held
    him tight.

And the people there still prattle – there is lots of
    tittle-tattle –
For they glory in the story, young and old folk, gold
    and grey,
Of how wicked treble Abel tripled trouble with his
    pebble,
But how Mabel (and some others) saved her brother
    and the day.

Alf Prøysen

MRS PEPPERPOT AND THE SPRING CLEANING

Illustrated by Björn Berg

IT WAS A BEAUTIFUL DAY in March. The sun was doing its best to melt the last remaining snowdrifts and cast a glow over the tall pine trees on the mountain ridge. Everything suddenly looked sharper and clearer in outline. Even the wooden walls of Mrs Pepperpot's house seemed to shine like polished tin. But when she looked at her windows she didn't thank the sun; it showed up how very dirty they were.

"Oh dear," she said to herself. "I can see it's time for spring cleaning again. Well, I might as well get down to it straight away, I suppose."

She went into the kitchen to get out her bucket, her scrubbing brush and plenty of soap and scouring powder. Mrs Pepperpot was pretty thorough when she got going – in fact, she enjoyed spring cleaning.

She was just about to start on the windows when she heard a slow buzzing sound over by the stove. A big black fly had come out of the corner where it had been sleeping.

"Oho!" she said. "So the sun's woken you up too, has it? Well, you needn't think I'm letting you lay eggs all over my house, making millions of flies to blacken my windows in the summer. I'll fix you!" and she rushed at the fly with a fly-swatter.

But the fly got away, because at that moment Mrs Pepperpot SHRANK!

"You wait!" she shrilled in her tiny voice, as she rolled along the floor. "I'll get you!"

"Don't worry," said a voice from the corner.

Mrs Pepperpot turned round; it was a large spider hanging by its thread from a web it had spun between the grandfather clock and the wall.

"Don't worry," said the spider, "I'll deal with that pest."

"You gave me quite a fright!" said Mrs Pepperpot. "I don't mean to be rude, but I've never seen you so close to before, and I didn't know you were so hairy and ugly…"

"I could return the compliment," said the spider, "but on the whole you look a bit better when you're small than when you're tramping round the kitchen in your great big shoes. Anyway, did you hear me offer to catch that fat fly for you?"

"Yes, I did," answered Mrs Pepperpot, "but I certainly wouldn't let you roll that poor creature up in your horrible web to be eaten for breakfast. No, indeed. If I had seen that contraption of yours before I shrank, I would have whisked it away with my broom!"

"Leave it to me!" said another little voice right behind her. This time it was a mouse.

"It's you, is it? And what d'you think a little scrap like you can do?" asked Mrs Pepperpot scornfully.

"Who's talking?" squeaked the mouse cheekily. "You're not exactly outsize yourself at the moment. At least *I* can run up the clock – hickory, dickory dock!" he laughed. "And then I can snip that web with my sharp teeth as easy as winking!"

"I'm sure you can," said Mrs Pepperpot, "but don't you see? That web is the spider's livelihood. Without those threads she couldn't catch her food and she would die."

"Well, in that case," said the mouse, "I suppose you're supplying me with *my* livelihood when you leave the cover off the cheese dish in the larder, hee, hee!"

"You little thief!" shouted Mrs Pepperpot, shaking her tiny fist at the mouse. "You push it off yourself, you and your wretched family. But I'll set a trap for you this very evening!"

"Did I hear a mouse?" asked another voice from the door. It was the cat. "Where is it? I'm just ready for my dinner."

"No, no!" shrieked Mrs Pepperpot, waving her arms at the cat, while the mouse was trying to hide behind her skirt. "You leave the mouse alone, you great brute, you. He hasn't done you any harm, has he?"

"Woof! Woof! Who's a brute round here?" The head of a strange dog was peering round the door. When he caught sight of the cat he darted after her, knocking Mrs Pepperpot over as he ran round the table.

The cat managed to get out of the door with the dog close behind her when, luckily, at that moment Mrs Pepperpot grew to her normal size! She lost no time in throwing a stick at the dog while Pussy jumped on to the shed roof. The dog went on barking till Mrs Pepperpot gave him a bone. Then he trotted off down the hill.

"Dear me, what a to-do!" thought Mrs Pepperpot. "But it makes you wonder; every little creature is hunted by a bigger creature who in turn is hunted by a bigger one. Where does it all end?"

"Right here!" said a deep voice behind her.

Mrs Pepperpot nearly jumped out of her skin, but when she turned round it was her husband standing there.

"Oh," she said, "I thought you were an ogre come to gobble me up!"

"Well!" said Mr Pepperpot. "Is that all the thanks I get for coming home early to help with the spring cleaning?"

"You darling man!" said Mrs Pepperpot, giving him a great big kiss.

Michael Rosen
DON'T PUT MUSTARD IN THE CUSTARD

Illustrated by Quentin Blake

DON'T

Dᴏɴ'ᴛ do,
Don't do,
Don't do that.
Don't pull faces,
Don't tease the cat.

Don't pick your ears,
Don't be rude at school.
Who do they think I am?

Some kind of fool?

One day
they'll say
Don't put toffee in my coffee
don't pour gravy on the baby
don't put beer in his ear
don't stick your toes up his nose.

Don't put confetti on the spaghetti
and don't squash peas on your knees.

Don't put ants in your pants
don't put mustard in the custard

don't chuck jelly at the telly

and don't throw fruit at the computer
don't throw fruit at the computer.

Don't what?
Don't throw fruit at the computer.
Don't what?
Don't throw fruit at the computer.
Who do they think I am?
Some kind of fool?

Grimm, retold by Naomi Lewis

THE TWELVE DANCING PRINCESSES

Illustrated by Lidia Postma

THERE WAS ONCE A KING who had twelve daughters, each more beautiful than the next, who caused him a lot of worry. To ease his fears, they all slept in the same room, their beds side by side, and every night the king himself locked and bolted the door. Yet, every morning when he unlocked the door he would find that their shoes had been danced to pieces during the night, nor was he able to discover how this happened. At last, he announced that any man who found out where the princesses went dancing could choose one for his wife and, what's more, be the next heir to his kingdom. But if a man came forward, then failed to solve the puzzle within three days and nights, he would lose his life. And that was that.

It wasn't long before a young prince presented himself to the king, and asked to try his luck. The king welcomed him heartily, and he was given a room adjoining the great bedroom where the princesses slept. There a couch was made up for him, and the door between the rooms was left unlocked. The prince settled down to his watch, but before long his eyes grew heavy and he fell soundly asleep. When he awoke the next morning the twelve princesses were fast asleep – but the soles of their shoes were worn into holes. The same thing happened on the second night and on the third.

"Too bad," said the king and he had the prince beheaded. Many more princes came to try their luck, but each one failed and each one lost his head.

At this time, there was a poor soldier, who was of no more use to the army

292

because of his many wounds. Tramping the roads towards the city he met an old woman who asked him what he hoped to find. "I hardly know myself," he laughed. "Perhaps I'll discover where the princesses dance away the night. Why, then I might even get to be king."

The old woman studied him closely. "That's not very hard," she said. "Just don't drink the wine they bring you in the evening, and then pretend to be fast asleep – and here's something else." She handed him a rolled-up cloth. "This is a cloak," she said. "When you put it on you'll be invisible, and so you can follow the girls wherever they choose to go."

The soldier had been joking, but the cloak and the good advice made him take the matter seriously. So he gathered up his courage and went before the king. He was greeted warmly, as the others had been; his rags were exchanged for princely clothes, and he was given the same adjoining room. As he was getting ready for bed, the eldest princess brought him a goblet of wine. But the soldier was cunning; he had tied a sponge under his chin, and let all the wine run into this, so that he didn't taste a drop. Then he lay down, and after a little while he began to snore as though he were soundly asleep.

When the princesses heard him they laughed. "There's another who doesn't value his life!" said the eldest. They began to open cupboards and boxes, pulling out gowns and jewels. Then they skipped about in their beautiful clothes, prinking before the mirrors. Only the youngest was distracted. "Do you know," she said, "I have a feeling tonight that our luck is out. Something is going wrong."

"Don't be silly," chided her eldest sister. "You're always worrying. You've seen enough princes come and go to know that there's nothing to fear. Why, this clod would have slept through even without the potion." Still, they looked once more at the soldier, but his eyes were shut tight and his breathing heavy and slow, and they felt safe.

Then the eldest princess went to her bed and tapped on it three times. It sank into the ground, and one by one the princesses disappeared through the opening, the eldest in the lead. Quickly, the soldier threw on his cloak and followed after the last and youngest down a flight of stairs. Halfway down, he stepped on the edge of her dress, and she stopped in fright. "What's that?" she cried. "Who's pulling at my dress?"

"Don't be a fool," snapped the eldest sister. "You must have caught the hem on a nail."

When they reached the bottom of the stairs, they emerged into a marvellous avenue of trees with silver leaves that sparkled as they moved. "I'd better take some proof," the soldier thought to himself, and reached up and broke off a branch.

The tree let out a terrible roar. "What's that?" cried the youngest princess. "I tell you something is wrong."

"Oh, for heaven's sake," sighed the eldest, "they're just firing a salute at the palace."

Next they came to a magnificent avenue of trees with leaves of gold, and finally to a third whose trees had leaves of glittering diamonds. The soldier broke a branch from each kind of tree, and both times there was such a roar that the youngest jumped and shook with fear even when the sound was gone. But the eldest princess still insisted that all the noises came from gun salutes.

On they walked until they came to a great river. Twelve boats were drawn up to the shore, and in each boat sat a handsome young prince. Each of the princesses went to a different boat and climbed on board, the soldier following the youngest. "I don't know why," said the prince, a little out of breath, "but the boat seems so much heavier tonight. It takes all my strength to row."

"Perhaps it is the heat," said the princess. "I feel quite strange myself."

On the other side of the river there was a brightly lit palace, and from it lively music could be heard. As soon as they were across, the young couples hurried into the palace, and through the night every prince danced every dance with his own princess. The soldier amused himself by

dancing too. And whenever a princess put down her goblet of wine he drained it dry, so that when she picked it up again it was empty. These games made the youngest princess feel more nervous than ever, but the eldest pooh-poohed her fears.

They danced until three in the morning, when their shoes were all worn through and they had to stop. The princes rowed them back across the river, and this time the soldier sat in the front boat with the eldest girl. Then, on the bank, the couples said goodbye to each other, and the princesses promised to return the following night.

The invisible soldier raced on ahead, up the stairs, and by the time the sisters came in, slow with exhaustion, he was snoring so loudly that they all began to laugh. "We needn't worry about *him*," they said, and after putting away their fine clothes and setting their worn-out shoes under their beds, they lay down and collapsed into sleep.

The soldier decided not to say anything to the king just yet, but to learn a little more about these strange goings-on. He followed the princesses again on the second and third nights, and everything was the same as before. The third time, the soldier took away a goblet as evidence. When the time came for him to appear before the king he took with him the goblet, and the silver, gold and diamond boughs.

The twelve princesses hid behind the door to hear what he would say. "Well," said the king, "have you discovered how my daughters manage to dance through their shoes every night?"

"As a matter of fact," said the soldier, "I have." And he told the king about the twelve princes and the underground palace, and brought out the branches and the goblet to prove his tale. When the princesses were sent for, they saw there was no use in lying and so they admitted everything. Then the king asked the soldier which princess he would like for his wife. "I'm not so young any more," said the soldier. "I had better have your eldest girl."

The wedding was held that same day, and the king declared that when he died the soldier would inherit his kingdom. As for the twelve princes, the spell they were under was lengthened for exactly as many nights as they had helped the twelve princesses to dance away their shoes.

John Agard
HAPPY BIRTHDAY, DILROY!

Illustrated by John Richardson

MY name is Dilroy,
I'm a little black boy
And I'm eight today.

My birthday cards say
It's great to be eight
And they sure right
Coz I got a pair of skates
I want for a long long time.

My birthday cards say
Happy Birthday, Dilroy!
But, Mummy, tell me why
They don't put a little boy
That looks a bit like me.
Why the boy on the card so white?

The Selfish Giant

OSCAR WILDE ~ RETOLD AND ILLUSTRATED
BY ALLISON REED

THERE WAS ONCE a giant who came down from the mountains to build himself a castle in the valley. All the people of the valley were amazed by the beauty of his castle and the garden that surrounded it. Flowers of every scent and colour grew there, and birds and butterflies flew everywhere. It seemed there was magic in the garden and in the afternoons after school the children would go there to play.

One day the giant dug up a tree as a present and set off up the steep mountain path to visit his friend. His friend was delighted to see him and the two giants sat talking for days and days. The giant told his friend all about his wonderful garden. "But surely," his friend said, "it cannot be the most beautiful garden in the world if you let all the children trample on it." And the giant saw some sense in what his friend said.

The next day the giants climbed to the very top of the mountain and found the biggest boulder anyone had ever seen.

"This will build a fine wall," his friend said.

And the giant set off home struggling under the weight of the enormous boulder.

After many days the giant reached the valley. With his left hand he smashed the great stone and laid the pieces one upon the other to build a great wall around the garden. It was autumn by the time the wall was finished. The giant stood back to admire his work and thought, "Now it really is my garden. No one will be able to spoil it."

Outside the garden, the children had nowhere to play. They wandered round the high walls when their lessons were over and talked about the beautiful garden inside.

"How happy we were there," they said to each other.

Winter came, and the garden was bleak and white and silent. The giant stared at the snow and longed for spring.

Months went by and there was no sign of a thaw. Little did the giant know that outside his wall the sun shone and the grass was green. Then one morning, the giant was woken by the song of a bird.

"At last," he cried, "spring is here."

He looked out of the window and saw that the snow was melting. In a corner of the garden the children had made a hole in his great wall. Laughing and shouting they ran happily into the garden. Everything came to life again. Flowers bloomed and the grass was green.

The giant hurried down to greet the children but when they saw him coming they ran away to hide. Only the smallest boy remained. He stood crying under a tree whose branches still had no leaves. The giant gently lifted him up and as the boy's small hands touched the branches the tree burst into blossom. "How selfish I have been," thought the giant. "With my great wall I have locked the spring out of my garden."

The children who had been watching came out from their hiding places. They shyly gathered round the giant and offered him flowers.

"It is your garden now, children," said the giant. And together they started to break down the great wall. With the stones they built arches and the children ran round and round and in and out of them.

The giant saw that his garden was more beautiful than ever. He loved all the children but he kept a special place in his heart for the smallest child. For it was he who had shown the giant how his selfishness had destroyed his garden. From that day until the end of the giant's life the children played happily in the garden.

Jack and the Beanstalk

TRADITIONAL ~ RETOLD AND ILLUSTRATED BY VAL BIRO

ONCE UPON A TIME there was a poor widow who had a son called Jack and a cow called Milky-white. All they had to live on was the milk from the cow. But one day Milky-white gave no more milk and the mother was in despair.

"Cheer up, Mother," said Jack. "We can sell the cow and then we'll see what we can do." So he took the halter and led Milky-white off to market.

On the way he met a gnarled old man with twinkly eyes.

"Well now," said the old man, "you look like a smart lad. I wonder if you know how many beans make five?"

"Two in each hand and one in your mouth," said Jack, as sharp as a needle.

"In that case," twinkled the old man, "here are the very beans themselves. They are magic, mind, and if you plant them overnight they'll reach the sky by morning. I'll swap them for your cow."

"Magic beans for an old cow! Now *that* was a good bargain," thought Jack, handing over Milky-white and pocketing the beans. He was sharp right enough.

"Beans?" shrieked his mother when he got home. "Five dried-up miserable beans for a cow? You are an idiot! Nincompoop! Dunderhead! Take that! And that! As for your precious beans, here they go out of the window!" She was beside herself with rage and sent Jack to bed without any supper.

So Jack shuffled upstairs, hungry and miserable.

But when he woke next morning he stared in amazement. His room was bathed in green light, shaded by great big leaves right outside his window. The leaves of a huge beanstalk that reached the sky! So the old man had been right after all.

Jack opened the window, jumped on to the beanstalk, and began to climb.

He climbed and he climbed and he climbed, until at last he reached the sky. And when he got there he found himself on a rocky road leading to a great big castle.

A great big woman stood there. Jack was hungry after his climb, so he asked her politely for some breakfast.

"Breakfast?" she boomed. "It's breakfast you'll be if you don't move off. My husband's an ogre and he likes to eat boys on toast!"

But she took pity on him, and led him into the kitchen. Jack wasn't halfway through his meal when thump! thump! thump! the castle began to shake.

"My old man's coming!" wailed the old woman and bundled Jack into the oven.

In came the huge ogre, sniffing.

"Fee-fi-fo-fum,
I smell the blood of an Englishman,
Be he alive or be he dead,
I'll grind his bones to make my bread."

"Nonsense, dear," said his wife, "you're dreaming. Just sit down and have your breakfast. You'll feel better then."

Well, the ogre had his breakfast, and after that he went to a chest, took out two bags of gold, sat down again and began to count. Soon he fell asleep, snoring enough to shake the rafters.

Then Jack crept out on tiptoe from his oven, put one of the bags of gold over his shoulder, and off he pelted. He climbed down the beanstalk, down and down, until at last he got home.

"Well, Mother, wasn't I right about the beans? They *were* magical, you see!"

So they lived on the gold for some time, but at last it ran out and Jack decided to try his luck again.

Up the beanstalk he climbed, up and up, until he saw the great big woman again.

"Aren't you the boy who came here once before?" she asked. "That very day my ogre missed one of his bags of gold."

"That's strange," said Jack. "I dare say I could tell you something about that, but I can't speak till I've had something to eat."

Well, the great big woman was so curious that she took him indoors and gave him breakfast.

Jack had hardly finished when thump! thump! thump! the castle began to shake again. "Quick!" said the woman and hid Jack in the cupboard.

"*Fee-fi-fo-fum,*" said the huge ogre sniffing around, looking very suspicious. But then he sat down to have his breakfast. After that he asked his wife to bring in the speckled hen, and she put it on the table.

"*Lay!*" said the ogre, and the hen laid an egg all of gold.

The ogre pocketed it, yawned and began to snore till the whole castle shook.

Jack crept out on tiptoe from his cupboard, took the speckled hen under his arm and ran away. But the hen gave a cackle and woke the ogre who began to shout. That was all Jack heard, because he was off and down that beanstalk like a shot.

Well, Jack and his mother became rich, what with a golden egg every time they said "Lay!" But Jack was not content, and before long he determined to try his luck for a third time.

So one fine morning he climbed up the beanstalk, and he climbed and he climbed.

And when he reached the great big castle he hid behind a bush until he saw the ogre's wife come out with a pail. Then Jack tiptoed into the castle and hid under the lid of a cauldron.

Thump! thump! thump! he heard and in came the ogre and his wife. "*Fee-fi-fo-fum, I smell the blood of an Englishman,*" roared the ogre and sniffed around the oven, the cupboard and everything, only luckily he didn't think of the cauldron. So he sat down to breakfast.

Then his wife brought in a golden harp and the ogre said, "*Sing!*" And the harp sang most beautifully till the ogre fell asleep.

Jack crept out on tiptoe from his cauldron, caught hold of the golden harp and dashed off towards the door. But the harp called out: "Master! Master!" and the ogre woke up just in time to see Jack running off.

Jack ran as fast as he could, but the
ogre came thundering after. He would soon have
caught up, only Jack reached the beanstalk first and started climbing
down for dear life. Just then the harp cried out: "Master! Master!" and
when the ogre heard this he swung himself down the beanstalk too.

By this time Jack had climbed down and climbed down and climbed down till he was very nearly home. But the ogre came down after him, came down and came down, and the beanstalk was wobbling under his weight like a jelly. So Jack called out: "Mother! Mother! Bring me an axe!" And his mother came rushing out with the axe and stared in horror to see the ogre's legs sticking through the clouds.

Jack jumped down and chopped at the beanstalk with the axe. He chopped and he chopped until the beanstalk was cut in two. With a terrible cry the ogre came tumbling down and broke his crown. There was a great big hole where he fell and the beanstalk came toppling after him. And that was that.

So what with the golden harp that sang, the speckled hen that laid golden eggs, and all that money, Jack and his mother lived happily ever after.

ACKNOWLEDGEMENTS

Every effort has been made to credit the material reproduced in this book. The publishers apologise if inadvertently any source remains unacknowledged.

NICHOLAS BAYLEY'S BOOK OF NURSERY RHYMES © illustrations Nicholas Bayley 1975. Reprinted by permission of the Random House Group Ltd.

QUENTIN BLAKE'S NURSERY RHYME BOOK © illustrations Quentin Blake 1983. Reprinted by permission of the Random House Group Ltd and A.P. Watt Ltd.

GOLDILOCKS AND THE THREE BEARS © The Hamlyn Publishing Group Ltd 1965. Reprinted by permission of Egmont Children's Books Ltd © illustrations Wendy Smith 1999.

HENNY PENNY text by Joseph Jacobs, amended and updated. © illustrations Nicholas Allan 1999.

THE THREE LITTLE PIGS © illustrations Rob Lewis 1999.

I WANT MY POTTY © Tony Ross 1986. Reprinted by permission Andersen Press.

A DARK, DARK TALE © Ruth Brown 1981. Reprinted by permission of Andersen Press and Penguin Putnam Inc, U.S.

'Pat-a-Cake, Pat-a-Cake' from A DAY OF RHYMES © Sarah Pooley 1987. Reprinted by permission of the Random House Group Ltd.

HALLO! HOW ARE YOU? Text © Shigeo Watanabe 1979 © illustrations Yasuo Ohtomo 1979. Reprinted by permission of the Random House Group Ltd and the Penguin Putnam Inc, U.S.

KING ROLLO AND THE NEW SHOES © David McKee 1979. Reprinted by permission of Andersen Press.

MR GUMPY'S OUTING © John Burningham 1970. Reprinted by permission of the Random House Group Ltd and Henry Holt & Company, Inc.

ALFIE'S FEET © Shirley Hughes 1982. Reprinted by permission of the Random House Group Ltd and HarperCollins Children's Books, U.S.

'Hickory, Dickory, Dock' from A DAY OF RHYMES © Sarah Pooley 1987. Reprinted by permission of the Random House Group Ltd.

IN THE ATTIC © text Hiawyn Oram 1984 © illustrations Satoshi Kitamura 1984. Reprinted by permission of Andersen Press and Henry Holt & Company, Inc.

THE SNOWY DAY © Ezra Jack Keats 1962, copyright renewed © Martin Pope 1990. Reprinted by permission of Penguin Putnam Inc, U.S.

'Twinkle, Twinkle, Little Star' from A DAY OF RHYMES © Sarah Pooley 1987. Reprinted by permission of the Random House Group Ltd.

THE WIND BLEW © Pat Hutchins1974. Reprinted by permission of the Random House Group Ltd and HarperCollins Children's Books, U.S.

'I'm a Little Teapot' from A DAY OF RHYMES © Sarah Pooley 1987. Reprinted by permission of the Random House Group Ltd.

WILLY AND HUGH © A.E.T. Browne & Partners 1991 Reprinted by the permission of the Random House Group Ltd and the Random House Inc.

'Granny, Granny Please Comb My Hair' from I LIKE THAT STUFF © Grace Nichols. Reprinted by the permission of Curtis Brown.

IT'S YOUR TURN, ROGER! © Susanna Gretz 1985. Reprinted by permission of the Random House Group Ltd.

'The Silent Ship' from THE BEST OF THE WEST © Colin West 1990. Reprinted by permission of the Random House Group Ltd.

DR XARGLE'S BOOK OF EARTHLETS © text Jean Willis 1988 © illustrations Tony Ross 1988. Reprinted by permission of Andersen Press and Penguin Putnam Inc, U.S.

'Geraldine Giraffe' from THE BEST OF THE WEST © Colin West 1990. Reprinted by permission of the Random House Group Ltd.

OLD BEAR © Jane Hissey 1986. Reprinted by permission of the Random House Group Ltd and Penguin Putnam Inc, U.S.

THE WHALE'S SONG © text Dyan Sheldon 1990 © illustrations Gary Blythe 1990. Reprinted by permission of the Random House Group Ltd and Penguin Putnam Inc, U.S.

JESUS' CHRISTMAS PARTY © Nicholas Allan 1991. Reprinted by permission of the Random House Group Ltd. and Bantam Doubleday Dell.

With special thanks to Klaus Flugge and the authors and illustrators of Andersen Press for their generous contribution to this anthology

First published in 2000

1 3 5 7 9 10 8 6 4 2

This edition © copyright 2000 Hutchinson Children's Books

Acknowledgements for permission to reproduce previously
published material appear on page 316

First published in the United Kingdom in 2000 by
Hutchinson Children's Books
The Random House Group Limited
20 Vauxhall Bridge Road, London SW1V 2SA

Random House Australia (Pty) Limited
20 Alfred Street, Milsons Point, Sydney
New South Wales 2061, Australia

Random House New Zealand Limited
18 Poland Road, Glenfield
Auckland 10, New Zealand

Random House South Africa (Pty) Limited
Endulini, 5A Jubilee Road, Parktown 2193, South Africa

The Random House Group Limited Reg. No. 954009

www.randomhouse.co.uk

A CIP catalogue record for this book
is available from the British Library

ISBN: 0 09 176878 0

Printed and bound in Singapore by Tien Wah Press [Pte] Ltd